SCREAMS FROM BEYOND THE CRYPT

Darkwell Bled (author)
Screams from Beyond the Crypt
ISBN 978-0-6489191-0-0

1. FICTION / HORROR
2. FICTION / SCI-FI
3. FICTION / THRILLER

Typeset Athelas 10/14

Cover illustration by Darkwell Bled
In-book illustrations by Laura Smith
Edited by Dr Catherine Heath AE

DEDICATIONS

To Andrew and Kate.
May only fictional horrors be found,
within your fairytale reality.

CONTENTS

NOISY
NEIGHBOURS

randon had been sitting at his desk for hours. The room was stale air, the only light emitted from a small over-taxed orange globe that had begun to double as a heat source. The windows were closed and the blinds were drawn. He could not allow himself to be distracted by the city below.

Tomorrow Brandon would have to submit a paper whose success or failure would determine whether or not his future in academia would continue. The essay, *his essay*, was due in the morning. Brandon had only barely begun to begin to write. His entire future was reliant on this paper, an essay that currently amounted to nothing more than a blank page.

Everything—his future career, and his future life—was dependent on his ability to think clearly, to rationalise, to concentrate and to craft an argument that a third-party observer would determine was sound and logical. It all hinged on tonight, and whether or not Brandon would be able to avoid procrastination, remain disciplined and undis-tracted, and manage to maintain his focus.

Yet, while all hung on such a delicate threshold, Mr Murphy, Brandon's upstairs neighbour, stomped and romped with unrestrained discourtesy.

He sounded as if he were marching. Back and forth, as though he were participating in some absurd military display.

Thump, thump, thump.

He, Mr Murphy, seemed like he was a military man. Ex-military, that is. An aged soldier, once a general, maybe.

Brandon had, in fact, never seen his upstairs neighbour, and only knew his name from the mail slots in the foyer. Even so, he could well imagine that this was exactly how he looked.

He, as he *stomped*, would be dressed in his ill-fitting general's outfit that had once made him look smart, the kind you saw in those old World War II movies. He was almost certainly wearing his old military boots. They were knee-high, black, and very heavy.

Thump, thump, thump.

This was absurd.

Brandon kneaded his fists into his forehead and tried to concentrate. Tomorrow would decide all. He needed to concentrate.

The essay requirements were simple enough: Here is your arbitrarily assigned topic. Are you for it, or against it? Defend your position.

But now, as he put pen to paper, he found he couldn't quite remember his position, or if he was for or against it, or what the topic was to begin with, and above him Mr Murphy continued his sick cruelties.

Thump, bang, groan, whimper.

It was a pitiful whimper.

Mr Murphy sounded as though he had stumbled, fallen over, hurt himself, and was now injured. He was no doubt drunk again, Brandon was sure of that. Brandon was certain that Mr Murphy was an alcoholic of the worst order, always on the sauce.

Or perhaps he had thrown something at his dog again, and now the poor creature, with its misplaced loyalties, was prostrating itself pathetically in the corner. Pets weren't even allowed in the apartment block, and Brandon had never seen one there—but Mr Murphy was the kind of person to blatantly ignore such rules, Brandon was sure.

The whimpering and the groaning merged into one and sounded more desperate and pained and Brandon was convinced that Mr Murphy was watching some kind of sick porn—some kind of torture porn with chains and kidnapping and unwilling participants—watched at such a high volume not despite the fact that his neighbours might hear, but specifically because they could and would, and because that's exactly the kind of sick thing Mr Murphy really gets off on.

Brandon re-read the question for the fifth time. He got out the dictionary and looked up each of the words that made up the sentence to make certain he fully understood them. Of course he did. He hadn't neglected his classes. Individually their meanings were perfectly plain, but when assembled in order they became jumbled and convoluted. No doubt it would make perfect sense with a clear head. With a clear head he would read it and think how it was all so obvious. It would be so much easier with a clear head, if he could just concentrate; it would be so much easier if Mr Murphy could just stop—what?

Rapping?—It sounded as though he were rapping his fingers on the floor, as if he were impatiently awaiting something. Brandon's essay, maybe? Perhaps Mr Murphy was somehow aware of the essay, and Brandon's struggle, and had chosen to mock him cruelly by rapping his fingers on the floor impatiently. Rapping them just so that Brandon would have to hear them rap and feel the time tick by as they did. Ticking down to the deadline, the deadline in the morning that would decide Brandon's fate.

Or was he *tapping* his foot softly, but incredibly fast? Or rapping and tapping all at once in order to somehow overlap the sounds that blurred into one another and became one and the same and yet infinitely distinct. It was white noise, static, endlessly bouncing back and forth, specifically manufactured for the purpose of distracting Brandon's synapses from firing; it was...

Vacuuming?—Maybe? It was so hard to tell, as the noise was so constant and yet so varied, and yet Brandon was sure a vacuum it must be. Mr Murphy was some kind of hypochondriac-neurotic, vacuuming at three in the morning, with no consideration for others and their schedules. All Mr Murphy could think of were dust mites and microscopic germs—but not people.

The essay had still not been begun, and with increasing certainty Brandon was becoming sure its topic had never been covered in class, and yet here its subject was clearly penned in his lecture notes, but he could not remember it, or the context of his notes, or how they related to the question, and yet he was sure he could figure it all out if Mr Murphy would just shut off his damn TV.

Yes, surely that's what it was: a *TV*.

Mr Murphy was doubtlessly an old man. He had Alzheimer's, and narcolepsy, and a bad hip. He had fallen asleep in front of the television, and the channel had ended for the evening, and it had gone to static. Not *vacuuming*, nor *rapping*, or *tapping*, but *static*—signal lost.

Well, that wasn't good enough.

Mr Murphy knew he was working on an essay, how couldn't he? Why would he be making such noise if not for knowing, and wantonly being cruel? Brandon's essay was due in the morning and his future depended on his concentration and his concentration demanded no distractions, and that required silence.

Brandon could stand no more.

Through the closed blinds the sun was shining, and the city below was waking, and Mr Murphy's inconsiderate cruelties still wouldn't cease.

So what if he were an old man, senile and fragile, or a perverted woman-hating dog-kicking sleaze to be avoided, or a veteran of World War II who fought the Nazis and deserved respect? Brandon was in the now and, whatever it was that Mr Murphy was, Brandon needed silence and Mr Murphy was refusing to let up with his incessant noise.

Brandon grabbed the broom from his kitchenette, and began banging on the ceiling above his desk. He banged, he thudded, and he began to yell:

"Hey, old man! Hey, general! Listen here, you neurotic hypochondriac sexual pervert!"

He slammed and he banged the broom head into the ceiling, and dust and paint and plaster rained down onto Brandon's desk and his unfinished yet begun paper.

"Stop your rapping and your tapping and your stomping and your vacuuming! Turn off your damn TV, and don't you know there are no pets allowed?!"

He cried and he hammered and he pounded and the tapping and the rapping became a thunderous downpour and the pathetic whimpering became squeals and screams and then finally the *crack*.

The ceiling that was Mr Murphy's floor gave way, and down onto Brandon's desk flowed a cascade of fattened well-fed rats that tapped and rapped and squealed and screamed, and with them slushed and rattled and sludged down onto Brandon's unstarted paper the few unfinished scraps and the gnawed bones that were once Mr Murphy.

MURDER ON ANAROK STATION

Detective Arek's position on Anarok Station was a formality more than anything else. One could not sneeze—let alone commit a crime—within the large deep-space facility without it being picked up on multiple cameras, microphones, and sensors, and then relayed to and through the facility's central brain. This brain—a synthetic hybrid of biological and mechanical engineering—linked all systems throughout the station into a hive-mind network that both managed and maintained all technical operations of the facility, as well as monitoring and observing all organic inhabitants. Despite this, Nexonian law clearly states that the process of law could not be left entirely to AIs, and so, with over nine hundred inhabitants living on Anarok Station, Detective Arek's position within the facility was deemed a necessity.

Crimes on a hive station, though inadvisable and uncommon, were by no means non-existent. They often took place in the form of regulation apathy, or crimes of passion; it was a being disregarding the airlock speed limit or an angry fight over a card game more often than not. Detective Arek's role in all this was a simple one. The crime would occur, the station's sensors would witness it, then the hive mind would collect, collate, and condemn as it saw fit. In all of this, all that was left for Detective Arek to do was to review, then sign off on, its findings. It had never been wrong, should never be wrong, and had always been entirely thorough and logical. In Detective Arek's ten years as the station's Naturally Formed Sentient Law-Enforcement

Officer he had never seen an incomplete or unsatisfying account of an offence come across his monitor. That was, at least, until now. It simply read:

Assault in progress—murder in progress.

The detective stared at the report.

It was, evidently, incomplete and furthermore had seemingly been sent to him while the crime was still in progress. There was no mention of who had been attacked, where, by whom, or when—all information that should be provided in a complete report (following an incident, not during). With the station spanning dozens of levels, hundreds of rooms, and nearly one thousand inhabitants, Detective Arek was somewhat at a loss as to what it was he should, or could, do with such information. It was, to begin with, unusual that his office would even be informed of an ongoing incident. His role was purely to deal with completed incidents, and it was down to the cogs—AI drones under the control of the hive mind—not him, to attend to ongoing offences. In light of this, in addition to the apparent possible murder, how and why he had been informed of the issue to begin with was a mystery in itself. Despite this, one thing remained clear: whatever the case was, clearly *something* was, or had gone, wrong.

Detective Arek considered the situation. On previous postings, before being assigned to this station, he would never have thought twice about following up on such a message. And it had *technically* come to him, even if it hadn't actually been meant for him. There was surely no harm in following up on it, even if all it led to was his learning that the hive mind had made a mistake, and that the cogs were already addressing the issue. Leaning forwards on his chair, he pressed down on the small button in front of his desk's holographic monitor and spoke:

"Computer. Against whom is the assault taking place?" he queried.

"Unknown," said the cold robotic voice.

"Where is, or where did it, take place?" he asked.

"No information beyond provided report is known," came the response.

"How can you report on a crime you don't know anything about?" Detective Arek muttered more to himself than he did to the monitor.

"No ongoing crimes detected," responded the voice.

Detective Arek let out a heavy sigh and, pulling himself to his feet, began to pace. When he had first been transferred to Anarok Station he hadn't trusted the heavy reliance on machines, but then, over the years, his convictions had been whittled down, and he had become complacent with the ease of his job. *Too complacent, perhaps,* he thought, and now he found himself in a situation where it looked as though he would have to actually earn his week's pay cheque. A crime had likely been committed—if that itself wasn't an error— and if a crime had not been committed, then whatever was wrong with the facility's hive mind would still need to be urgently solved. Whatever the case was, today Detective Arek found himself with a most unusual puzzle to investigate. A puzzle in which the first point of concern was not *who* had committed a crime, but instead *whether* a crime had been committed and, if so, against whom.

It occurred to him that while there was no time stamp on the report, as transfer of information on the station should be nearly instantaneous, the arrival of the report itself on his monitor may suffice. He stopped pacing, turned back to the monitor, and pressed down on the small button once more.

"When did—" he began, but was stunned into silence by an explosion—or impact—that shook the entire station around him and knocked him off his feet.

Pulling himself up and quickly moving towards the window of his small office, Detective Arek looked out into the blackness of space and half expected to see that they had fallen under attack. He had heard rumours of Roaming Nation pirates out this far, and had even heard of them coming to blows with the Nexonian Navy, so their hitting a civilian station was not impossible. His fears, however, slowly relaxed into confusion. There was, so far as he could see, nothing but stars. No other ships were in their vicinity. Just blackness, stars... and then debris.

Like a morning mist rolling over the mountains, slowly Detective Arek became aware of a cloud of mangled mechanics, metal and corpses floating away from the obscuring bulk of the station that widened beneath him. They tumbled through zero gravity, cold, silent, and dead.

Several levels below him, many of the facility's inhabitants had just been sucked out into the cold vacuum of space.

Detective Arek swore in several tongues that he was not fluent in and, turning away from the window, marched back to his desk and the button.

"What caused the explosion?" he demanded.

"No explosion detected."

He paused. Sometimes the hive mind required annoying levels of exactness.

"What caused the... damage to the station?" he tried.

"No damage detected."

More swearing.

Something had clearly gone wrong, and people had died. He had seen the bodies, and yet his monitor seemed to have no knowledge of the situation whatsoever. Pulling on his belt and holstering his side-arm, Detective Arek moved to leave his small quarters. The door hissed open, and on the other side he found pandemonium.

The lights were intermittently flickering—possibly damaged by whatever had gone on downstairs, though that seemed unlikely as they were so many levels above. Organic sentients of many species were running down the hallway in frantic fear. He grabbed the long thin arm of an Aldayyan as it attempted to run past; he pulled it aside and demanded answers.

"What's going on?" Detective Arek questioned.

The Aldayyan—a species known for their sky-blue complexion complete with wispy white cloud-like markings that slowly move across their skin—had turned nearly transparent out of fear. Detective Arek could see the creature's lungs inflating and deflating, dark-black blood pumping, and hearts beating rapidly.

"The station's gone mad!" it spat.

"I see that," said Detective Arek, "But what has caused you all to act mad?" he asked, annoyed.

"Not us! The station!" it yelled, twisting its arm out of Arek's grip. "There was an explosion, the lights are flickering, and life support is down! I'm getting off while I still can!" it said, turning and resuming its path down the hallway, towards the nearest life pods.

Detective Arek tilted his head and strained his ears past the immediate commotion in an attempt to hear the telltale hissing of the station's life support system. There was none, and for a moment he allowed himself to wonder if life support was just down in this hallway, or if it had been down in his quarters too, or whether the issue was station-wide. Life support not functioning was, in itself, not an immediate issue. There was enough oxygen on the station to last weeks, and the cogs would have it fixed by then, but it was perhaps emblematic of a larger problem at hand. However, how this was all tied together, Detective Arek was not at all certain. His pondering was broken by dull thuds which could be felt reverberating through the floor of the station, attesting to the fact that, indeed, life pods were being launched, and many people were alarmed enough by the apparently wide-spread goings-on that they were evacuating themselves from Anarok Station.

With haste Detective Arek moved towards the station's nearest elevator. There was clearly a problem, and though he had no idea what it was, he was becoming increasingly sure it was tied to whatever had happened down below. Someone had apparently been attacked, but who and by whom was not clear. An explosion or impact had occurred, but how, why, and whether it was connected to the assault was also not clear. The elevator doors closed behind him, and Arek allowed himself a moment of pleasure in finding that at least this system seemed to be functioning. Then the robotic voice asked his intended destination, and Detective Arek considered; the most likely solution to his problems was that the causes of the assault and the explosion were in fact one and the same. It was conceivable that someone had killed someone, and that their death had resulted in the explosion—killing a heavy-vehicle operator while they were behind the controls, perhaps. Whatever the case, as the two incidents had occurred so close together, it was more likely that they were linked than it was that they were unrelated, so the location of the explosion was the most logical place to focus his investigation. However, beyond the vagueness of it having taken place below his quarters, he wasn't exactly sure on what level it had occurred, and the system—when asked—had seemingly had no knowledge of any issue whatsoever.

Suddenly an idea occurred to him.

"Computer, has usage of this lift increased recently in passenger numbers beyond average?" he asked.

"Affirmative; usage up five hundred and thirteen per cent over usual daily traffic at this time," it confirmed.

"From which level did this spike in usage first occur?" he pressed.

"The increase began on Level Three. This cabin was filled in excess of recommended weight and unit capacity by several times its limit," it said.

Detective Arek nodded, satisfied. If Level 3 was the place people had first begun fleeing, then that was where the issue had taken place.

"What is your destination?" the computer repeated.

"Level Three," Detective Arek ordered.

The hallways of Level 3 were eerily quiet. As home to a large hangar bay, the third level of Anarok Station would usually be bustling with trade and travel. It now—devoid of the rabble of sentient life, and absent of life support's ambient hissing, was completely silent. All the main doors to the hangar were sealed—something that should only occur in an emergency—and with growing apprehension Detective Arek found himself becoming increasingly certain that it was this main hangar whose former occupants were now littering space. He approached a door and activated its comm system.

"Does the hangar bay have atmosphere?" he asked.

"No issues detected."

Detective Arek glanced uneasily towards the silent ventilation system. The monitor in his quarters had not reported that life support was down and had not known about the explosion. The hallway monitor here seemed equally unaware of the lack of life support in the hallway. Its failure to detect *any issue* did not exactly instil in him confidence in its ability to determine whether or not there was atmosphere in the room beyond, regardless of how interconnected the hive-mind system *should be*. Detective Arek paced back and forth, and found himself wishing he knew more about computers. All areas of the station were equipped with maintenance cogs, so chances were that if atmosphere had been lost in the hangar bay, then it should by now have been restored. However, by that same nature, cogs should have also restored life support, which they evidently had not. If there was a breach, and the breach remained, then opening the door would result in his being vented into space along with the others. This prospect did not in the least appeal to him; however, opening the door was also, so far as he could figure, the only way of discovering what was going on. Taking a deep breath, he braced his back against the wall of the hallway, crossed his fingers, and ordered the door to open.

Upon the door opening, the atmosphere in the hallway did not explosively decompress, and Detective Arek let out a long sigh of relief.

Within the hangar, all was returning to normality. The breach that had evidently existed in the hangar's outer doors had been patched with heavy sheets of metal, and maintenance cogs were going about performing several smaller repairs. Detective Arek approached a pair of these drones, intent on getting to the bottom of the day's strange events.

"What happened here?" he asked.

"Unknown," said the first drone.

"The hangar doors failed to open for an approaching ship—there was a collision," said the second.

Behind them Detective Arek watched as two identical cogs unevenly lifted a heavy crate, with one drone applying force a half-second before the other. He returned his glance to the two supposedly integrated drones that evidently had uneven knowledge. Systems supposedly connected across the entire ship were unable to relay or detect the simplest pieces of information. Maintenance drones were unable to coordinate even the most basic of tasks. It was in this moment that Detective Arek realised he had all the evidence necessary to conclude both who had been killed and where.

Making his way back to the elevator, Detective Arek took the lift to the centre of the facility, where one would find both the proverbial heart, and literal brain, of Anarok Station.

The entrance was guarded by two security cogs, and, though he realised it would likely be futile, Detective Arek (cautious that the killer may still be behind the door they guarded) paused and attempted to gain information.

"Who is behind that door?" he demanded.

"Unknown," said the first cog.

"You don't know who is in the room of the central brain?" Detective Arek asked.

"We are... suffering from individuality," admitted the second cog reluctantly.

"Yes, I know," agreed Detective Arek as he drew his side-arm.

"Open the door, and be ready for combat," he instructed.

The two cogs, drawing weapons of their own, moved to flank him, and the door to the central control hissed open. The floor of the room beyond was slick with neural lubricant and odiously foetid with the rank smell that so unusually and uniquely belonged to synthetic mechanical/biological hybrids.

The killer was gone, but the victim was still present.

The dome containing Anarok Station's central brain was shattered, its brain stuff smashed and obliterated.

Cables and flesh were strewn about on the walls, the floor, and the ceiling—dripping black ichor and green coolant.

The brain was dead, the hive mind ended, and the victim found.

Anorak Station had been murdered.

THE BOY IN
THE TREE

Peter loved to walk in the midnight warmth of November streets. Night-time never seemed so dark in the summer. The warmth burned away all precipitation from the air—Adelaide was rarely humid—and, in the dry heat of a November night, the stars and the moon provided Peter with what felt like a second day—one that seemed magical, and privately his own.

There were no winds, and there were no people in his midnight domain, and Peter allowed his thoughts to roam freely as he trudged through the streets. He had no destination in mind—to wander aimlessly through the night was his very goal.

Some houses he passed sprang to attention with porch lights and dog barks, but most remained dark, docile, and lifeless. There were the occasional glowing windows with open blinds and Peter unapologetically glanced in as he walked by, seeing men asleep on couches and TVs performing brightly to their inattentive audiences. One house danced with pretty fairy lights, and Peter wondered if they were early Christmas decorations, very late ones, or were simply always there—and he appreciated them regardless of their reason.

He passed down an unlit walkway walled on either side by an eight-foot fence of corrugated iron, and came out into an old cul-de-sac that he had never been in before. These homes were rich, stately, and dark. Their great gardens were gated from the road and wildly overgrown. More than a few had inoperable fountains and algae-covered ponds. This was, Peter thought, no doubt once the most elegant street in town, and likely still the wealthiest. But it looked as though its owners had aged, become less capable of upkeep, and much of it had fallen into disrepair.

Peter walked and saw that some homes had sheets for curtains, and wondered if they were still actually inhabited. The homes were all two storeys or taller, and each distinct in character but well suited as a collection. Towards the end of the cul-de-sac Peter paused to observe an overgrown cherub statue, and was startled by a black cat that darted from some gated-off chest-high grass. It darted past him, and his eyes tracked it as it ran onto the next property (the last on the street), and disappeared into yet more tall grass.

The garden into which the cat had run belonged to a house that was the biggest on the street by far, and perhaps the most dilapidated. Despite its extreme state of disrepair it *did* appear to be lived in, evidenced by a small light flickering dimly from a third-floor window. There were statues of gods sticking out from the grass, and a large long bush that was doubtlessly once a well-groomed hedge. Rising to the height of the building's second storey was an impressive apple tree that bore no fruit, and on one branch that stretched out at around Peter's own head height was the small dark figure of a boy.

The child statue immediately caught his attention, and Peter stuck his head through the bars of the gates to observe it closely. He had never before seen a statue placed in a tree, and admired the creativity of whoever it was that had placed it there. He then found himself taken aback by the morbid nature of the statue, which appeared to have a rope placed around its neck, then found himself frightened when it seemed to move, and horrified when it dropped and hanged itself.

For a moment Peter stood frozen in shock as the figure swung with the inertia of the drop. The feet kicked slightly, and Peter sprang into action. Someone had just hanged themselves. Some kid, some young boy, had just hanged himself. Peter pushed through the gates. They weren't locked, but they were rusted, and the grass had grown against them; pushing with all his might only opened them a sliver, but a sliver was enough. Going through sideways he edged past the gates, waded through the grass, and ran towards the apple tree, stooping on his way to grab a pair of rusted hedge clippers that stuck out dangerously from the ground.

Reaching the tree he began to cut at the rope. The blades of the clippers were heavily rusted, and what should have been a single snip became many. Then he was hacking at the rope with the clippers, and then he sawed at it, working to free the figure—the child—the young boy from his self-fashioned demise. Finally the rope gave way, and broke in two, one half bouncing upwards, freed from the weight, and the boy with the other half silently dropping to the dirt and grass below. Peter struggled to release the bindings from around the boy's neck and, when he had finally loosened them enough, the child gasped for air.

Peter automatically embraced the boy with compassion and concern, crying out, "Good god, good god, are you okay?"

After the boy had stopped gasping he pushed Peter away, and demanded in his small voice that Peter "quit his fussing".

The child was a tiny runt of a boy, with dark black hair and pale skin, and pale eyes to match. In the moonlight he looked damn near translucent, and Peter found himself wondering if the child had ever been touched by a ray from the sun. The boy became annoyed by Peter's scrutinising stare, and so spoke up again.

"Quit your staring," he said.

Peter was taken aback. "Are you okay?" he asked.

"Fine," the boy said shortly.

"What were you thinking, using a rope such as you were?!" Peter demanded, throwing the freed rope into the grass. "You could have died!" he said, though he was sure that that was likely the boy's intention.

The boy stood up and kicked the ground slightly, his pale eyes refusing to meet Peter's.

"I was just messing," the boy quietly replied, before turning to leave.

Peter followed him. He did not believe the boy was, as he said, "just messing", and feared that he fully intended his actions, and was further fearful he may attempt them again.

"Where are you going?" Peter asked from two steps behind.

They were walking past the apple tree towards the side of the house, seemingly towards a cellar door that stood open. The magic had gone from the evening, and now Peter looked at his overgrown surroundings and the strange boy not with fascination, but with fear. What would a boy so young as him be doing in a place like this, at this time of night? The boy stepped into the cellar and took two steps down while Peter remained at the entrance.

"Where are you going?" Peter repeated.

"To bed," the boy replied. "It's late, you know?" he added, and the cellar doors slammed behind him.

The cellar door was locked. Peter pulled, pushed, and banged on the cellar door to no avail. It was definitely locked.

Peter was unsatisfied. He—to begin with—couldn't believe the boy actually lived in a place such as this, nor could he believe the child's intentions towards himself were not dangerous. For a brief moment he considered calling the police. They would surely send someone—child services, or something. But then he remembered the dull light on the third floor. A parent, maybe? Whoever it was either knew the child and should be told what he had tried, or didn't know the child and should be informed that a child had locked himself in their cellar.

Moving back around to the front of the house Peter hammered on the front door to no avail. He then tried the doorknob—it wasn't locked.

Entering the home, Peter felt like a trespasser—he supposed that, in reality, he was. But desperate times called for desperate measures, and he felt sure both the police and the occupants would understand. Calling out his presence as he walked the halls and climbed the stairs, Peter couldn't help feeling a little unsettled by the overgrown exterior and the dark dusty interior of the large old home.

Every stair creaked from ground to third floor, and, as he passed the levels he saw nothing but dark hallways and closed doors. Furniture covered in dusty drop sheets. Cobwebs that were themselves so old that they had been abandoned. It wasn't until Peter reached the top floor that he saw anything different: a single open door, and one dim light.

This was no doubt the room that shared the window he had seen from the street. Peter called out again with a "Hello?", but this time it was a whisper, not a yell. He was no longer certain he wanted to be heard, and was nervous of what sort of person (or creature) would live in a house such as this one. He feared what he might find in the room, and memories of old movies he had seen as a child filtered through his mind, suggesting to him encounters with vampires, werewolves, and monsters and their mad doctors. With a deep breath he braced himself at the threshold and then stepped through into the light, only to find a dusty old chair, and an old dead woman.

No, she wasn't dead. Just sleeping.

She was asleep, and she was old. A copy of *Robinson Crusoe* was open spine-up on her lap. The light flickered from the orange bulb of a standing lamp that looked as though it had been on its last legs two legs ago.

"Um," said Peter, unsure of how to proceed.

"Who's that—what?!" cried the old woman, sitting up and suddenly awake.

"Ah—hello," Peter said dumbly.

"If you are here to rob me, you should know I've lost my purse," the old woman responded, and Peter wasn't sure whether or not she was joking.

"No, no; I'm not—there is a boy downstairs," he began to explain.

"Yes, yes, William..." she said sleepily, settling herself back down into the chair.

"William? Is that the boy's name?" Peter asked, unsure whether she meant the child, or if she, in her confusion, thought that *he* was William.

"William is my twin brother," she said slowly, her eyes now closed.

The boy looked no older than eight, and the woman looked no younger than eighty. If she meant the boy was William, then clearly she had gone very senile.

"There is a boy in the cellar. I'm worried for him. Do you have a key?" he tried again, fighting to stay calm and unannoyed.

"Oh, don't worry about William; there is no sense in worrying about William," she yawned.

Peter was growing vexed.

"Look," he said, "If you do not give me the key... I will have to call the police... The boy has already tried hurting himself," he tried to explain.

The woman sighed heavily, and grunted her way to her feet. She grabbed keys from where they sat on her bedside table (right next to a purse) and she began to slowly shuffle her way out of the room and down the hall.

"Bother an old woman," she said. "Wants to waste the nice policemen's time," she added. "Doesn't he know it's long past midnight?" she questioned. "No sense of civility," she concluded.

Peter followed her slow progression down the stairs and out the door, and as she shuffled she didn't let up from commenting on Peter's character for a moment.

"Probably a thief," she theorised. "Probably after my purse!" she accused. "Good thing it's lost," she reflected.

They were now passing by the apple tree and heading around the side of the house to the cellar. Peter pointed to the branch with the half-rope that remained hanging from it.

"The boy was trying to hang himself," he again tried to explain, "and your purse is on your side table," he added.

"William is always trying that; tried yesterday, and will try tomorrow, I'm sure," she grunted as she crouched down towards the door of the cellar and began fumbling with the keys. "Never works, though," she added.

"It might have worked tonight had I not cut the rope," Peter said, both angry and revolted by her cavalier attitude towards the boy.

"Nope, it's never the rope; cut it did you? I did too! It doesn't matter. It's never the rope. I bet you forgot his gun, though?" she said remorsefully.

A shot rang out. Peter jumped, but the old lady seemed unfazed.

"Thought so," she said.

With a heave the old lady pulled the heavy cellar doors open, and the smell of gunpowder escaped the room and assaulted Peter's nostrils. The lights flickered on, and revealed a dust-filled bedroom that looked as though it had gone unoccupied for half a century or longer.

"There's—there's no-one here...? But I heard a shot?" Peter stuttered.

"Yup, you missed his gun alright," said the old woman. "I did too that first time," she added regretfully.

THE MANGROVES

The mangroves of St Kilda are a vast tangle of low canopies, twisted roots and branches, saltwater puddles and ponds, and occasional dry salt shelves. Once a popular tourist location, the grove's boardwalk has long since fallen into disarray and disrepair. In 2015 this state of dilapidation saw a metal gate erected, closing off more than half the boardwalk to the public. This gate included a sign that stated *Closed Due To Maintenance*; however, by 2030 this closure had begun to appear indefinite. In addition to this first sign and gate, another was eventually erected at the boardwalk's entrance. This second sign, however, did not speak of maintenance, but instead warned of prosecution for trespassing under the Summary Offences Act of 1953.

Despite this, the boardwalk and its tangled groves were still frequented—albeit illegally—by a new crowd. This group consisted mainly of urban explorers, schoolboys looking for a thrill, and teenagers hoping for a private place to drink and together be alone. Because of the illegal nature of these adventures, the mangroves were now almost exclusively visited under the security of night's darkness, and it was within this veil of secrecy that rumours were fostered and spread.

From these forays there were—as the local newspaper would eventually put it—whispers of "things that go bump in the night". Sensationalist as the talk of Big Foots, monsters, and aliens was, none could deny that since the boardwalk's closure a surprising number of tall stories had come out of the dark forest. These tales were never verified, and their sources—unwilling to put themselves at risk of a fine—were never named. In the long tradition of urban mysteries, most of these accounts were said to have happened to "a friend of a friend", though those willing to claim them as their own in social settings would fervently hold to the stories' sincerity.

Eventually these stories reached a level of notoriety that warranted the police to comment. They laughed at the idea of monsters and pointed out that South Australia was far too far from North America for Big Foot to have travelled. The "alien lights", they suggested, were nothing more than the fires of those who were regrettably choosing to camp illegally. Mostly the police simply laughed off the claims and warned against trespassing; however, their acknowledging the stories at all proved to do more damage than good. The next morning's local paper reported the response with a front-page headline that stated *"Police Address Concern over Mangroves Aliens and Monsters"*, which immediately caused the rumour mill to reach new levels. It was this headline that also finally inspired Duncan, Paul, and Maria—who had been following the rumours from the mangroves for over a year—to jump the rusted fence, disregard the unevenly hanging sign, and begin down the rotted wooden platforms of the St Kilda Mangrove Trail's boardwalk.

"What do you reckon they are?" asked Maria, taking in the amber evening sunlight that shone through the low-hanging canopy over the boardwalk. The boards beneath her were rotted, and gave noticeably under her footfall despite her petite build.

"Birds," replied Duncan simply, eliciting an annoyed explosion of air from Maria's nostrils. Maria was a true believer in the supernatural. She was (she proudly claimed) "a real Mulder", an *I want to believe poster* hanging in her bedroom-office and all. Duncan was not.

"Come on, Dunk! There've been three weird occurrences this month! And that's just the ones we've heard about! How can you say it's just birds?!"

Duncan laughed and took her hand. The small silver ring she wore was cold but quickly warmed to his touch. Maria and he had been dating for two years now, and engaged for one, and this kind of passionate uproar was exactly what he had hoped to elicit with his comment. He took immeasurable pleasure in stirring her up—but just a little.

"Monsters," he finally agreed. "Monsters, ghosts, goblins, werewolves, mummies, vampires," he elaborated.

"—And lions, and tigers, and bears, oh my!" Paul added from behind.

Paul had crouched down to take a cinematic photo of them walking along the path's wooden boards. Each plank appeared to be perpetually damp despite the dry, warm evening, and some showed the blackness of rot through them. A few had begun to break away entirely, and almost all of them were peppered with small divots of unclear origin—as though someone had been walking the trail while wearing soccer cleats. His camera clicked loudly and on its display screen Paul could see that he had managed to snap a good action shot of his two friends in mid-step. The three of them had been going on their "ghost adventures" since long before Maria and Duncan had begun dating, and Paul remained the comfortable third wheel to all their non-romantic outings.

Maria was the team's enthusiast and researcher, and the only "true believer" amongst them. She had founded the group back when they were all still in high school. Her room looked as though it was the office of a detective in a mystery film, with sticky notes covering the walls and pins of different colours marking spots on local maps denoting sightings of various creatures. She had read every book and article on local hauntings, and had penned several blogs on the matter herself to her small but enthusiastic following. Paul was the documentarian and photographer of the group. He had yet to see or photograph any ghosts or monsters, but he had captured a whole lot of pretty scenery and interesting buildings, and so he was content. He had no strong belief in ghosts, neither positive nor negative, but often answered "There were no white swans until there were" when he was pressed on the matter. Duncan was just there for the ride, and the company more than anything else. He was an unabashed cynic, who did not believe in ghosts, spirituality, magic, or religion, but enjoyed their adventures and the atmosphere of their outings all the same.

"Don't fall too far behind, Paul; it's getting dark real fast!" advised Maria, quickly glancing down at her wristwatch.

She had had the watch since she was eleven, and on its face a cartoon Scooby-Doo was pointing one arm at the seven and the other at the twelve.

Paul laughed. "It's getting dark fast, so don't walk too far ahead!" he called back in response.

Maria and Duncan had walked about twenty metres along the boards, talking offhandedly about the various rumours Maria had collected in regards to the location, when suddenly a loud click and a bright flash lit up behind them, signifying that it was officially dark enough to warrant Paul to begin using his camera's flash.

"Caught any of the Universal Monsters yet, Paul?" jested Duncan.

"Just the Invisible Man... but I can imagine the Gill-Man might be around these parts," he responded dryly.

The sun hung close to the horizon but, with the thick canopy of the mangroves surrounding them, darkness was encroaching far more quickly than the sun was setting. Fearing that they would soon find themselves in total blackness, the trio decided it was time to establish their camp. They were not exactly spoiled for choice. With the tide having come-in, many of the flat areas that would have been dry when their walk began had already flooded—or soon would. A quick look around gave them only two strong options: a small mound of salt shelving slightly off of their path, and a two-benched gazebo that the boardwalk cut through the middle of.

Both the salt shelf and the gazebo had their positives and negatives, not the least of which was the risk of a foot-wetting presented by the encroaching tide. However, with the heavy presence of mosquitos and the unsealable nature of the gazebo's structure, it was decided that the group (in violation of the posted signage requesting visitors not to leave the boardwalk) would step off the path and establish their tent roughly fifteen metres away from the trail. Their tent, once built, stood in a location almost entirely encased in the twisted knots and branches of the surrounding groves.

"Are you sure that this area won't get wet?" Paul asked as he took a snap of their small camp.

"If it isn't wet now, I think it will remain okay," Maria replied.

The trio planned to take full advantage of their long weekend, and stay until Monday evening. Because the sightings were all reported as having happened at night, it was intended that they would sleep through the day—their tent shaded by the groves—and then explore all night. However, before they set out on their first night's adventure it was decided that dinner should first be had, and bug spray should be liberally applied in preparation.

"One of these is more than your daily recommended salt intake," Duncan read with dramatic false concern from the back of his packet of two-minute noodles.

"Full of salt, surrounded by salt, sleeping on salt. When in Rome, et cetera et cetera," replied Maria as she poured the last of the Pringles from the tube into her mouth.

"See the mangroves; be the mangroves," added Paul, who was intermediately eating Doritos while looking through his photos.

"Any mysterious shapes in those?" asked Maria with true hopefulness.

"No, they're all triangles," responded Paul.

"I meant in the photos, not the Doritos," said Maria,

"Oh—well, no; what shapes are you expecting to see?" he responded without looking up.

"Pygmies," she said, drawing Paul's attention and now stopping his scrolling.

"Pygmies," repeated Paul in disbelief. "In South Australia," he continued, not phrasing it as a question.

"Isn't that term derogatory?" asked Duncan.

Maria reddened. "It is the proper anthropological term!" she replied with exasperation, before adding with hesitation, "I... looked it up before we left."

"This boardwalk was made in 1984; don't you think a supposed *tribe* of people would have been seen when, or since, they built it?"

"They have been seen! Two of the weird occurrences reported this month spoke of 'little people' running around in the mangroves, and there is an Aboriginal myth of small people, 'red devils', that were here, they say, even before the Indigenous people were!"

"Well, if 'pygmy' isn't offensive, I'm certain 'little people' or 'red devils' is," replied Duncan.

"Oh, be quiet," replied Maria with a laugh, throwing her empty Pringles tube in his direction.

"I'm just saying, dear, in this modern political clima—"

"Shhh," she said, now whispering.

"You wouldn't want to—" Duncan began again before Maria once more cut him off mid-sentence.

"No, really, shut up; listen!" she hissed.

The trio fell silent, and somewhere in the distance a soft sound like nails being driven into rotted wood could be heard plodding along the boardwalk.

Maria's breath caught, lines of concern ran across Duncan's face, and Paul cut the power of their small travel lamp, plunging the tent into darkness. The plods continued, grew in number, and were soon accompanied by the splash of water and the crunch of sand.

"... some kind of animals?" Paul whispered in suggestion.

"Whatever it is, there are a lot of them," Maria whispered fearfully. She had seen one too many adventure films set in the exotic and largely fanciful Africa of Hollywood and, between them and the theory she had just postulated, it was all too easy to imagine that they were surrounded on all sides by a savage tribe of minuscule mask-wearing spear-wielding cannibals.

"Whatever they are, I don't care, so long as they're not parkland security," hissed Duncan.

Behind them, somewhere in the darkness, branches broke and crunched with sudden closeness. Maria screamed, a powerful odour filled the tent, and Duncan burst out laughing.

The tent's travel lamp flickered on and Duncan struggled with the tent's zip before stumbling outside gasping.

"I don't care how many monsters are out there; I need fresh air!" he yelled.

"Dunk, don't!" Maria called after him, to which Duncan replied, "I have to! Don't worry, there's nothing out here; your fart scared them away!"

Maria joined him on the outside, pouting.

"Girls don't fart!" she said with faked indignation.

"See? Nothing here," Duncan repeated.

Paul, joining them on the outside, glanced around then snapped a shot of the mangled branches behind their tent.

"Nothing here now, but *something* was," he concluded.

Their following investigation confirmed this. In addition to the broken branches, they could see that small cone-like divots had been pushed into the sand, forming a trail that returned to the boardwalk and joined the hundreds of similar punctures in the wood that Paul had previously observed. The dents, both in the sand and the wood, were photographed by Paul, and a vote was put forward as to what their next steps should be.

"Well, we go home, or we push on. It is as simple as that," Duncan laid out.

"We can't go back; this is something, for once *something!*" Maria voted, not allowing her initial scare to deter her.

"I agree; after years of us doing this, this is some kind of tangible lead and, even if it is just a herd of nocturnal possums, I'd like to know," Duncan stated, turning to Paul for his vote.

"All possums are nocturnal," Paul replied, adding, "Well, it will be nice to have something to actually photograph for once."

It was decided, and so the trio glanced up and down the boardwalk and the trail of pinpricks going off in both directions.

"Which way?" Duncan asked after a pause.

"Deeper," Maria responded. "The boardwalk is a full loop—we'll have to jump another fence to do the loop—but at least if we go deeper, we won't backtrack, and we won't miss anything," she suggested.

"Deeper," Paul responded, flicking on his flashlight. "Good," he added with false enthusiasm.

Maria and Duncan activated their flashlights in turn and all three of them began to plod along the path.

They walked in silence, jumping at every shadow, and pointed their lights at every sound the wind made throughout the darkened canopy above. The moon was only half full, and the night cloudy; in the blackness they walked with quiet caution.

The boardwalk on which they slowly progressed ran only 1.7 kilometres through the thick groves, but to walk the full circumference around the twisted trees would be to journey 44 kilometres. Within the 1,219 hectares of thick forest in which they now found themselves, it was easy enough to imagine that somewhere an entire lost civilisation of undiscovered pygmies could exist. Maria was thinking that actually discovering a lost tribe—or, even more unbelievably, an actual cryptid—would make hers a household name. Duncan was thinking that perhaps he had been a little too early to cynicism, and that maybe, just maybe, he was a little scared. And Paul was thinking that he had to take a shit.

"I have to take a shit," Paul said.

"Really?!" Maria responded, annoyed by the potential delay.

"Yeah, I've gotta," he confirmed.

Duncan threw him a roll of toilet paper from his backpack as Paul stepped off the boardwalk into the trees.

"May the bear spirit protect your call to nature," Duncan called after him in a poor imitation of a Native American accent.

"Don't go too far!" Maria cautioned.

"But don't stay too close!" Duncan requested.

Maria fidgeted with her silver ring with impatient anxiety.

"What if we actually find a something?" she asked.

"Well, then Paul photographs it," said Duncan simply.

"And if they're dangerous?" she prompted.

"Well, then Paul photographs it, and we run," returned Duncan.

As they conversed, the scent of fresh air and sea salt was once more drowned out by the unnatural odour that they had suffered in the tent.

"I guess I owe you an apology; smells like Paul was the perpetrator of that chemical attack earlier."

"I'll look for your retraction in tomorrow's paper," replied Maria.

Before Duncan could mount a witty retort of his own, a loud crack broke from the trees and Paul shrieked, then went silent. Maria and Duncan ran towards the noise. Upon arrival at the location of the shriek, Duncan vomited at the odour's revolting explanation and Maria paled.

Paul was gone. In his place was nothing but broken branches, his camera, and a severed arm.

Duncan, in hysterics, stood dry-heaving against a thick branch.

After a moment, Maria regained her composure somewhat, but was still unsteady on her feet.

"It's not his," she concluded.

That was for damn sure.

The arm was rotten and had clearly been in a state of decay for days or possibly weeks. It was apparent that it was a contributing factor to the foul smell, but by no means made up the whole of it.

"That's an arm!" Duncan reported loudly, shakily pointing towards it.

"Yes..." Maria replied, snapping a shot of it with Paul's abandoned camera, before crouching near the limb to take another photo from a lower angle. It wasn't just part of an arm, but a whole arm, all the way up to the shoulder joint. Maria noted, with a fascination for detail that made Duncan feel all the more unwell, that the arm appeared to have been chewed off rather than cut, as the flesh around the shoulder joint was torn and uneven. She then inspected it from another position and found something further that was unusual about it.

"The end of this arm is hollowed out, like something dug around in it, or was jammed into it," she reported, and Duncan vomited again.

They walked further into the darkness of the tangled mangroves, and away from the footpath. Had they still the option to recast their vote, they would have both opted to turn back and go home. With Paul now missing that was, however, no longer an option. The flashlights gave them little visibility amongst the claustrophobic branches, and the moon had entirely given up on them. They splashed through shallow ponds and tripped on winding roots, inadvertently but unavoidably announcing their presence to anyone who cared to know of it. Maria and Duncan felt sure that there were those out there who *did* care to know, and they could feel the eyes of these strange predators watching them, and stalking just beyond sight.

"Paul would never leave his camera," stated Maria.

"Paul also wouldn't disappear mid-shit into the forest in the middle of the night," replied Duncan.

"That isn't funny," Maria criticised.

"It wasn't a joke," replied Duncan weakly.

They had been wandering for half an hour when Duncan's flashlight flickered, and went dark. What followed happened with a speed that attested to how closely and patiently their stalkers were watching them.

Maria's torch smashed—knocked out of her hand by an unseen projectile. She screamed, and Paul's camera (which she had still been holding) went off, its flash momentarily stunning Duncan. Burned into his retina by the flash, though quickly fading, was the dark strobe-captured image of dozens of small creatures. They were chest-high figures of strange obscurity. Duncan blinked rapidly and the short monsters slowly faded as his sight was restored back to normality. The odour returned, Maria shrieked and yelled again, and Duncan was knocked to the ground, hitting his head, and losing consciousness.

Duncan could not be certain upon awakening exactly how long he had been unconscious, though the lingering odour convinced him that it had been, at most, minutes. Maria was gone and the flashlights were scattered and broken. Feeling around on the forest floor, Duncan soon found Paul's camera and, using its flash as a light source, he managed to eventually stumble and tumble his way back to the boardwalk. Where he arrived was not the spot from where they had left the path, so he looked around to familiarise himself with his surroundings.

In one direction the path continued as it had been; this was, he thought, where they had come from. In the other stood one of the boardwalk's observation posts, rising up above the groves. Figuring that this was his best option for finding his friends, Duncan moved quickly towards the observation post, climbed the wooden ladder that led up to the tree-house-like platform, and began to scan the horizon.

From this vantage point it would be, Duncan lamented, very difficult to see his friends, who were no doubt obscured by the thick canopy. It would, he was sure, be even harder to see the small creatures that the camera's flash had briefly burned into his vision.

Duncan paused in thought.

It *was* the flash of the camera that had burned the image of the creatures momentarily into his eyes... Had the camera in doing so managed to capture an image of them?

Duncan brought up the camera's display screen. The camera was on low battery following his use of the flash as a light source, and so, not wanting to waste any further power, he pulled up the latest photos hastily. Duncan looked at the screen, and a small demonic creature—captured in perfect HD—looked back at him.

"Woah, Paul and Maria will be rapt with this photo," he said, before realising the sad irony of the statement.

His best friend and his fiancée were lost somewhere in the forest—likely taken by these strange creatures—and Duncan fully intended to find them. He looked down again at the image. There were three of them photographed—one staring directly at the camera and two caught mid-stride. The creatures (aside from their bipedal nature) did not appear to be human in any real sense. Nor were they the red devils of Aboriginal legend—or at least not insofar as that name referred to the creatures' colour. Rather than red, the three small monsters in the photograph were of the same hue as the salt plains that had birthed the mangroves, and perhaps had birthed these creatures too. They stood (from what Duncan could tell by the photo) no higher than four feet tall. However, *stand* may be too loose a use of the word to describe what these creatures did.

Balanced was perhaps more accurate, as these demons were footless. While their thighs and knees looked as they should, beyond the knee joint the creatures' anatomy took a horrific turn. Their legs ended in sharp spikes that ran from the shins and tapered into narrow points ending where their ankles should begin. These points appeared to sink deep into the sand, apparently leaving the dents and holes that Duncan and his friends had earlier observed. In addition to the leg spikes the creatures were similarly without hands, with spikes tapering from their forearms towards the place where their wrists should start. Their eyes were deep, sunken and black, and their teeth were seemingly filed sharp and of a similar darkness. Were it not for their strange limbs, their faces alone would inspire terror, but as a whole they were, as a collective, dread itself.

Duncan, despite his years of dating Maria, had never heard described anything to match creatures such as these.

The image of them raised more questions than answers, and Duncan began to ponder their strangeness to himself.

He wondered whether or not their sharp limbs were from a deformity, or if they were natural, or a cosmetic cultural modification, like foot binding.

And what of the severed limb they had found when Paul had gone missing? Was it one that one of the creatures had lost through leprosy or some such similar disease? Was that why their arms looked the way they did?

This seemed unlikely. The three creatures caught in the image had spikes tapering from their forearms towards their wrists, whereas the severed arm was detached high up at the shoulder.

In that case, he wondered, had they brought the severed arm with them? Or perhaps it was unrelated. Had Paul simply screamed at seeing the arm, and was it that noise which had attracted them?

This didn't seem likely to Duncan either. Paul was never squeamish—although it was true Duncan had never seen him exposed to something quite so gory.

But if the arm hadn't already been there, then why would the creatures bring it with them?

This question scared Duncan the most. Perhaps the creatures carrying a severed arm indicated that they were cannibalistic, though it did seem strange to him that they would bring with them something such as an arm on a... a what? *A conquest? A hunt?*

Maybe the arm was meant as a club, Duncan thought, but that didn't explain why (as Maria had noted) the end of it had been hollowed out. Nor did it explain how creatures with no fingers could use a club... or even carry one, or carry his friends off, for that matter. At the very least, what was clear to Duncan was that the creatures were evidently hostile and that, whatever their intentions towards his friends were, he must find Maria and Paul as fast as he could. However, in an area as vast as the mangroves, what was far less clear to Duncan was exactly how he should go about doing such a thing.

It was only at this ponderous impasse that Duncan's thoughts cleared enough to allow him to hear his surroundings. Somewhere below, in the distance, and moving away from him were the crashing sounds that had twice earlier signified destruction and odour. Duncan quickly turned off the camera to conserve its battery and, standing upon the lookout, cast his eyes out across the forest. He scanned the tangled branches of the groves, at first seeing nothing, but was drawn to a stop by strange movements in the distance. There were, pushing and breaking through branches, three lumbering figures of unusual height and disjointed movements. Their arms and legs seemed to bend in more joints than was natural. In stark contrast to the little demons he had witnessed earlier, these creatures appeared to stand perhaps seven feet tall and, with extraordinarily long low-hanging arms, they walked with a strange jolting lumber. They appeared to be moving towards an orange glow in the distance that could only just be made out through the trees, and Duncan immediately marked their destination as his own.

These creatures were, Duncan reasoned, *surely* connected in some form with the smaller ones. After all, what were the chances of two unknown monsters existing within the same forest? Further, much as they were crashing through the mangroves now, similar crashing had been heard in relation to when both Paul and, later, Maria had gone missing. What's more, these creatures were possibly an explanation for how his friends had *actually* been taken as, while he couldn't imagine the small handless creatures managing to carry a person, he could certainly imagine one of the tall ones achieving it. These larger creatures were perhaps subservient to the smaller ones, Duncan reasoned, or perhaps vice versa. At the very least it seemed they shared some form of symbiotic relationship with one another, as there had been evidence of both of them at each of the encounters they had had.

Despite these larger creatures' long legs, and despite his running through near pitch-blackness, the tall monsters lumbered with a slowness that allowed for Duncan to gain on them in short order. Soon, he found they had reached their destination, and so he stopped too. Reactivating the camera, Duncan observed them through its zoom from a distance. From this presumed safety and obscured by trees, Duncan looked in on the strange village, and any doubt that these giants were connected to his small attackers or his missing friends were immediately eroded.

The two tribes were clearly one and the same, with the three large creatures he had observed from afar standing amongst the smaller ones. They all appeared as dark ill-defined shapes in the night, lit only by a small flickering fire in the centre of their encampment. He could not see his friends, and this worried him immensely, because the creatures moved with excitement and there was nowhere else he could imagine his friends to be. Beyond that, even with the camera's zoom, any further details were impossible to make out. They were too far away, and it was too dark. Hoping to approach further, Duncan switched off the camera again, only to immediately realise he was no longer alone.

It was the smell that did it. That odious stench of rank and rot that three times earlier had alerted him to the presence of these large creatures. Before Duncan had even had a chance to move, he felt a cold hand close itself over his throat and stifle his yelp. It closed and he could feel that the hand was dirty, bloodied, and ice cold. He kicked and writhed to get loose but, for his efforts, was thrown hard against a nearby root, which thudded softly with indifference. Once more he was rendered unconscious.

Duncan awoke and was immediately reminded of his position by searing pain and the stench of rotting flesh. A sharp-toothed creature—one of the minuscule ones—was biting and tearing at Duncan's upper thigh. He kicked at the creature with his free foot until it scampered away, only to be replaced immediately by two more. They ripped away at his flesh, tearing his skin to threads that hung loose and bloodied, and in a strange moment Duncan found himself noting that they comically resembled the rubber of a burst balloon.

At this range he could see the creatures in even clearer detail.

The sharp endings to their limbs were exposed bone, spiked to a point. Whether natural or not, Duncan could not tell, nor at this point did he much care. At the section in which the bone connected back to flesh their skin was fused directly to it, and clear stems of exposed nerves hung freely from their joints.

Duncan tried to convince himself that there were no clear signs of his friends in the encampment. He reassured himself as best he could, that the bloodstains on the salt shelf and the two skulls and torsos burning in the flames of the small campfire could belong to anyone—*the person who had earlier lost an arm, perhaps.*

Duncan kicked and screamed and thrashed as more of the small creatures piled on to him. A few used their spiked limbs to pin him down through impalement. They tore at his upper thigh, and bit into his shoulders at the joints.

He was losing a lot of blood, and his vision was blurring, and he was growing tired. *Just so tired.*

Defeated, and utterly exhausted, Duncan turned his head to the side and tried to think of anything but his own cannibalisation.

Nearby he saw one of the giants, and an explanation for their absurd size and strange disjointed movements became clear.

These creatures, the large and the small, were *definitely* one and the same.

He could, in horror, just make out the shine of Maria's silver ring on the creature's hand, and her watch on its wrist.

That explains why there are only skulls and torsos in the fire—an unacknowledged voice noted somewhere deep inside Duncan's mind.

Her hands, her arms, her legs: now the creature's.

The towering monster of dead flesh that wore Maria's arms and legs had, until recently, been one of the smaller creatures. Where its arm and leg spikes should have been, Maria's arms and legs began—explaining the creatures' extreme height, their long limbs, and their unnatural additional joints.

It shifted its weight, and lumbered across the encampment in a strange jumble of movements—still unaccustomed to its newly obtained limbs.

Duncan felt his own leg torn free at the thigh and, moments before the pain took him permanently into the darkness, he saw one of the small demons jam its leg spike into his severed limb, and deftly wriggle its toes to familiarise itself with its new extension.

ANGRY EYES

There was a moment of blackness, and then the living room.

Daryl Pepperton could not remember where, when, or how he had met his wife—only that he loved her dearly, and that tonight she would die. The kids had gone to bed, and would never awake, and soon he and his wife would settle down to watch television. They would channel surf and settle on *Jeopardy*, where, by the end of it, the fourth-night champion would lose. Soon afterwards Daryl and his family would die.

Die, be killed. Murdered viciously.

Daryl was not sure why he so assuredly felt this would be the case. He could not explain the knot of fear that had tied itself inside his stomach, or the anxiety that dripped cold sweat down his back, or why while surrounded by such love and pleasantries his thoughts refused to turn from dread and disaster. There was, so far as he could think, no catalyst for these thoughts—they just were, and perhaps always had been, and always would be.

Martha Pepperton sat beside Daryl where she always did, and always would, and Daryl watched her pretty lips move and her eyes smile. How completely he loved her, and their life, and how he longed to hear her voice over the panicked throbbing in his head. He concentrated hard, and distantly heard her ask what they should watch, and from far away he heard himself answer, "*Jeopardy.*"

The show ran on, and though he had no answers Daryl felt he had heard every question before. It was a repeat; *all of this was a rerun.* His wife smiled and spoke words she had said before, and Daryl nodded in agreement just as he had the last time, and the time before that, ad infinitum. Every moment reeked of déjà vu, and every conversation felt as hollow and distant as an echo.

Martha poured a glass of wine that she had drunk before, and above them two silent thuds exploded loudly. Daryl felt himself ask what the noise was, but before any answers could be given or known, he had already begun to mourn and acutely feel the death of his children. It burned with an intensity beyond their singular loss, and was accompanied by every time they had died before, or would again, and was compounded by the limitless helplessness of Daryl's existence.

And then *he* entered. The man with dark hair and angry eyes. The man who would and did soon shoot Daryl's wife. Martha reached out to Daryl, and Daryl to her, but before they touched he too was shot. His death was not instant, and as he lay bleeding out he found he could fully fathom the cruelty of the crime, the unfairness of the deaths, and the tragic slaughter that was the end of the Pepperton family. Daryl Pepperton was dead.

He was dead, and soon awoke in a room of mirrors. From all angles of the room stared back at him angry tired eyes and dark hair become grey. The face of the killer. *His face.*

Memories flooded back—a lump-sum payment, his breaking and entering, shooting the children as they lay sleeping, and then shooting Martha and Daryl Pepperton in their living room. There was more: his running, his capture, his subsequent arrest and trial. And now he felt their suffering just as acutely as he recalled himself having caused it.

And then a cold disembodied voice spoke: *"Scott Franks. Crime: Murder, first degree. Four counts. Sentence: Life in prison subject to Empathic Neural Stimuli."*

The man screamed and writhed in full understanding and remembrance of his position.

How many times must he be forced to be and to love those whom he has killed?

How long was he cursed to live and experience the actions of his own cruelty?

Suddenly Scott Franks felt the reality of his existence begin to distort as his memories blurred and became manipulated.

His own self-identity and awareness twisted, and all sense of time and being became uncertain.

It would all soon begin again, just as it had for decades.

"Victim Sympathy Simulation will commence again momentarily."

There was a moment of blackness, and then the living room.

Daryl Pepperton could not remember where, when, or how he had met his wife—only that he loved her dearly, and that tonight she would die.

CLEAN-UP, AISLE THREE

Amanda sat on the counter in silence. The sun would rise soon and the morning staff would start to arrive, but she knew they would be too late. There was nowhere to go, and there was nowhere to run.

Amanda closed her eyes and thought back to how it all had started.

The night had begun slowly, and seemed no different to any other midnight shift at Bargain Sales before it. In a town so small as theirs it was uncommon for them to have patrons at such a late hour. Were it not for the fact that their store was part of an international chain whose rules and opening times showed bureaucratic indifference towards the needs of the location, they would surely stay open no later than 6 pm. As it was, this was not the case, and so from 11 pm onwards the skeleton staff of the small grocery store were visited by few—mainly drunks, either heading to, or leaving the town's nearby pub.

It had just turned 2 am and Bethany (a member of the floor staff) had gone on her break. Amanda was manning the counter, Raymond (the manager) had not been seen for at least forty minutes, and Micky was taking the unnecessary time to make sure all labels were facing forwards while putting out stock. There were only four staff members on from 11 pm to 6 am, and the store was almost entirely silent— they had long since turned off the instore jingles—and all that could be heard was the soft *tap, tap,* of Micky placing cans of beans onto the shelves.

Twenty minutes passed. It had so far been an uneventful evening. There were still no customers, and so Amanda was attending to her nails, and Micky was working with purposeful sluggishness knowing that (as there was so little stock to put out) if he were to complete his task, he would be left with nothing else to do. Vaguely Micky was aware of the sound of the two automatic glass doors sliding open at the front of the store, and of the footsteps that stumbled through. He was, however, not bothered by them. Customer service was Amanda's job, and he was, after all, on his knees unloading cans of beans.

Amanda did look up from her task but still said nothing. She watched as the man dragged his feet into the store with a directionless trudging. He walked as though he were an extra in a George Romero film; she couldn't tell if it was tragic or comedic, and decided it was probably both. The man had a vacant expression, could barely walk, and smelt like a two-days-dead rat stuck in the wall on a summer's day. Amanda breathed a sigh of contempt knowing that this was something she would have to deal with. In silence she watched him lumber past the counter, hoping that he would simply realise that this was not the pub, and just go home, but when he started to moan loudly she decided it was time for action.

"*Micky…*" Amanda pleaded whiningly, looking from the man to the stock boy.

Micky, despite hearing this, gave no response. *If she really needs my help, she can walk over and ask me*, he thought.

"*Mickyyyy...*" she pleaded again.

He continued to ignore her, and continued to stack beans.

"*Micky!*" she said, this time shouting.

"What?!" Micky finally yelled in response.

"We've got another one," she said dramatically.

"So?" he responded with indifference.

"So make him leave!" she cried.

The man was clearly off his head, and gave no response, verbal or otherwise, to this back and forth. Micky sighed heavily.

It was the company's unofficial policy that the night crew had several male staff members in order to prevent theft and remove undesirables. This rule, official or otherwise, had never made sense to Micky, a nineteen-year-old stick insect of a boy who would never be described by anyone as "the muscle". It also annoyed him that he was expected to do what wasn't in his job description, and work as security, without receiving a pay cheque for it.

"Get Raymond," he responded, pointedly not looking up from the shelf of beans he was restocking.

"Raymond is taking a dump," she shot back, annoyed.

Despite being their manager, Raymond was not much older, and not much more competent than either of them. On a slow night shift, equipped with a cell phone capable of playing games and watching movies, well, Raymond was almost always "taking a dump".

"Raymond is always taking a dump," Micky grumbled.

The intruder, moving again, swayed his way past the counter, and stumbled halfway towards the aisle in which Micky was crouched. Suddenly the man began to whine and moan loudly, causing Micky to jump.

"Please Micky, he's drunk and it's making me un-com-for-table," Amanda whined from the counter, taking time to draw out the last word. She was complaining loudly enough for Micky to hear, and yet seemingly went completely unnoticed by the man.

Micky sighed again, and, wiping his hands on his black nylon pants, stood up to assess the situation. It had never really been Micky's intention *not* to kick the man out. He had done it countless times before, and usually with very little altercation. More often than not they would just insist that they were here to buy a snack, and once escorted from the chips aisle with more salted goods than any one man should consume in a single sitting, left without further fuss. Still, regardless of how many times he had had to do it, and how little issue it usually was, Micky didn't intend to ever do it without at least a facade of protest. He figured that, as it wasn't in his job description, then he'd better make a show out of doing it, lest they begin to expect it of him without thanks. The interloper groaned again and Micky finally turned to him, and was shaken by what he saw.

The man was horribly pale. His eyes were sunken deep into his head, and the whites of them had turned a dark yellow. They jittered in place as though they were unable to focus on any one thing. He smelt bad—*real bad*—and as well as his groaning there was from within him—despite his jaw being locked shut and firmly set—a strange noise like chattering teeth.

Cold sweat ran down Micky's spine.

This guy was obviously far gone. Off his face on some sort of substance. Micky had heard stories from an older stock boy of the time a meth head had trashed the store. It had taken three of them to fight him off, and one had ended up in hospital. Micky was just here for beer money while he went through university, and he had no desire to be beaten senseless by a druggie. He swallowed the lump in his throat dryly, and attempted to find a safe non-confrontational way to request the man to sod off.

"Umm," he eventually eloquated.

At this the man began to shake. Shakes which quickly turned into shivers, and then into impossibly fast vibrations, before the man fell backwards, hitting the hard tiled floor with a sickening *thwack*, and becoming still.

The moment the man had connected with the floor his odour had instantly worsened, and a loud hiss, like steam escaping a valve, was heard. The smell was rank with thickness, and Micky threw up on the shelved beans.

"What happened? Woah, are you okay?" Amanda asked, coming over.

Micky was still dry heaving at the smell, and recovered only enough to wipe the spittle from his mouth with his sleeve and yell for Amanda to call an ambulance, and for Bethany to get off her break and to bring over the first-aid kit. Fighting to regain composure, he pulled his shirt up over his nose in an attempt to mask the smell and began to inspect the man closely.

He was surely dead, Micky thought, noting in disgust a large crack that ran down the side of his head, showing bone beneath and blackness within. There was no blood, but Micky was unsure whether this was a bad sign or a good sign, remembering that once when he had cut his finger badly enough for stitches, it hadn't bled at all for the first few seconds of the injury.

Micky's inspection was cut off when Bethany ran over with the first-aid kit.

"Figures we get this crap while I'm having my dinner," she muttered, annoyed. "I'm not counting this as part of my break," she added.

"I think he's dead," said Micky.

"Are you a doctor?" Bethany responded sarcastically.

"Are you?" Micky cruelly shot back.

Bethany blushed with hurt and anger, as Micky's comment hit its target directly. He knew full well that, had she not failed her last semester of university, she would indeed be well on the road to becoming a doctor. But an almost-doctor was not a doctor.

"I will be by this time next year," she muttered under her breath, before checking the dead man's lack of pulse.

"Woah, I think he *is* dead," she agreed.

Suddenly the door to the bathroom slammed open, causing both Bethany and Micky to jump.

"Who's dead? What the hell?!" Raymond demanded, drying his hands on the back of Micky's shirt. Suddenly his face twisted as the smell hit him like a physical wall.

"*Jeeeesus*! What's that?!" he coughed, clasping his own shirt to his face.

Micky quickly caught both Raymond and Bethany up on the situation, pointing out the crack in the man's head, and theorising that it was that which had killed him.

"Well, are any of you chuckleheads going to call a damn ambulance?" Raymond diligently demanded.

"Little too late for that," replied Bethany.

"He's dead, you see," added Micky.

Raymond blinked twice. "Right. Sure, but then—well, then, call the police!" Raymond suggested instead.

As their discussion carried on, Amanda moved down to join them, store phone in hand.

"No luck on the ambulance; the call wouldn't go through," she reported.

"He's dead, Amanda. An ambulance won't help him! Call the police!" Raymond ordered.

"It's the same number, Raymond," Amanda spat back.

Raymond swore, and began pacing. When he had been given the job of night-shift manager two months earlier he had been told it was a "tremendous responsibility" and had been asked if he was sure he was up to the task. At the time he had assured the store manager that he could handle it; now there was a smelly corpse lying in front of his bean aisle.

"That number should never be down, Amanda. Are you sure that you dialled it correctly?" questioned Bethany.

"It is three zeros, Bethany; it isn't exactly complex maths," Amanda replied sarcastically.

"Well, there was that one time on the register wh—" began Bethany, planning to bring up a particularly embarrassing memory, when the strange chattering began anew.

"—When you, when you..." she tried to continue. "Where is that coming from?" she said, giving up on her dig.

"I think it's coming from him..." Micky said, motioning towards the dead body. "He was doing it before..." Micky trailed off.

"...before he died," Amanda added softly.

Suddenly the chattering went silent and, after a pause, a loud crack rang out that sounded as if someone were shelling an especially large peanut, and the smell worsened. Bethany, still kneeling beside her patient, uttered a befuddled "What?" before scampering backwards into the shelving behind her. A moment later those that were standing all took an involuntary step backwards, as the crack in the man's head widened.

It was like watching a chicken be born of a rotten egg. The crack in the skull lengthened and led to further cracks, that pushed outwards and were barely (and sometimes not at all) held on by thin, struggling strips of skin, which tore, and once torn allowed fractured bone to fall to the floor. There was no blood that came from the man's head, just black mush, even as the skull fell open. For a moment no-one was sure what they were looking at. Then, from the shattered skull, a long spindly stalk short forth. Slow and quivering, it was followed by several more stalks that—as they extended—pushed away further parts of the skull, and further widened the hole in what was once a man's face. These stalks found their place, and bent and latched on fast to the surrounding head. They bowed inward, and from their middle to which they joined, rose out a central mass— an arachnid-like torso encased in a crustaceous outer shell. The creature was black in colour, eyeless, eight-legged like a spider, had two additional feelers like an insect, and was covered in a thick textured carapace like a crab. Once fully emerged it jolted from the man's skull with impossible speed and left behind nothing but a hollowed-out blackened bowl where once the man's brain had sat.

The creature skidded on the smooth tiled floor, ran directly into a fixture, and then disappeared behind the aisle's long shelving.

"Christ in a cupcake, what the hell was that!?" Raymond shouted.

"I'm getting the hell out of here," Bethany stated. She stood, walked towards the glass doors, and screamed.

Beyond the automatic doors, and along the glass-walled front of the store, dozens of further creatures could be seen scuttling about. Some were in the distance, briefly illuminated by the streetlight across the road, and others could be seen more clearly illuminated by the light of the store.

Several ran aimlessly into the glass front of the store or into the doors, only to dart off in a separate direction.

Luckily they appeared to be either too light or too small to cause the automatic doors to open, but Raymond was taking no chances. The creatures might not be able to open the doors, but those infected by them certainly could. Quickly, in an attempt to prevent any more of these creatures or their carriers from making it inside, he ran over and with the manager's key he had hung around his neck, he both disabled the door's censors and locked them. Micky then slowly approached the locked doors, and closely examined one of the strange creatures that ran against them. It had dark yellow-orange markings across its back like many poisonous creatures do. Its crustaceous outer shell looked hard, and its legs looked sharp.

"Wouldn't want to step on one of these bastards," Micky observed.

"Mmmhmm," responded Bethany quietly.

"There is still one of those *things* in here," Amanda said with concern.

"It came from inside his head," Bethany whispered, looking towards the aisle and the body.

It was fairly clear that the creature was dangerous. Things that are good for human mortality don't generally burst from their skulls. And so, with effort, they somewhat regathered their wits, armed themselves with brooms, and sat on the raised safety of the front counter to discuss their next move.

"We can't call the police, and we can't leave," Amanda reported.

As she spoke they saw the creature scuttle out from under one aisle, bang into a chocolate bar stand, change direction, and then scuttle behind another.

"They don't appear to be especially bright," Micky noted.

"We should catch it," suggested Raymond.

"We should stay the hell away from it," retorted Micky, Amanda quickly agreeing with a whisper of "Yes."

"It may be a new species. If we catch it, there might be money in it," said Raymond.

"It exploded out of a guy's head," replied Micky, entirely unconvinced.

Suddenly, like an elastic band snapping, Bethany seemed to come out of her daze.

"I'll help catch it," she offered brightly to the stunned silence of the others.

No-one gave a further response for a few seconds. Micky looked from the creatures outside the window to the corpse down the aisle, and shuddered at the sound of movement somewhere in the store.

"Well, you can count me out," he said definitively.

"Uh-huh," agreed Amanda.

Bethany turned to regard them. Knowing it would be far more difficult for her and Raymond to catch it alone, she attempted to mount her argument:

"Look, this thing *did* come from that guy's head, and it could be some kind of new species. I mean *I've* never seen anything like *that* before! Maybe it's a kind of parasite or something that no-one has ever heard of. One that grows in people's brains, and then kills them, and then spreads."

In truth Bethany didn't really want to put herself in danger, nor did she care about Raymond's hope for a reward (not that she would turn one down were it offered) but instead figured that capturing such a creature—*one completely unknown to medical science*—would be a feather in the cap of her currently unimpressive academic career. It may even force her professors to allow her to return to university following the unfortunate "plagiarism" misunderstanding that had seen her expelled last semester.

"Well, if it is a brain parasite, then I am *definitely* out. I'm not getting exposed to a brain parasite, not for minimum wage," responded Micky.

"Sure," agreed Bethany amicably, "unless we are already exposed. For all we know we might be. Maybe it spreads by that smell we smelt; maybe we inhaled some airborne particles or whatever. Who knows? And, if we are exposed, then not capturing it could be a death sentence, and capturing it may be our only chance of diagnosis," she reasoned.

"Yes, exactly!" agreed Raymond. "Plus, reward!" he added.

Before either Micky or Amanda could give an answer, their thoughts were interrupted by a loud crash in the third aisle, signalling that the creature had knocked over the dog-food stand. Bethany and Raymond rushed towards the disruption with brooms in hand, and Micky reluctantly trailed behind. They arrived in the aisle just in time to see the creature run headlong into another fixture, before darting off in another direction.

"They're blind," Micky noted aloud.

"Hey, yeah, I think you're right!" agreed Bethany.

"If they're blind, they should be easy to catch," reasoned Raymond.

The creature re-emerged from under the store's fixtures once more, this time going towards the back-left corner of the store, where, due to the freezer units for food and drink, there was nothing under which it could conceal itself. It bounced between the two walls that made up the corner as if it were a Roomba caught in a loop, and Raymond and Bethany slowly began to approach it from either side, with Micky hanging far back between them.

"What are you going to do from back there?" yelled Raymond.

Stay alive, Micky thought, but instead said, "Cut off its escape when it gets past you two!"

Raymond grumbled something about cowards and slackers, and then, having drawn close enough to the creature, brought the broom head down hard upon it.

Until the broom connected with the creature it had been facing towards the wall, but on connection it quickly swivelled to face Raymond, and began making the same strange clicking noise they had heard emanate from within the dead man's head. Raymond froze—the broom still resting on top of the creature—unsure how he should proceed, and uncertain why he believed a broom would stop or stun a creature that was covered in a protective shell.

"Raymond, mate, maybe we should regroup and rethink this," suggested Micky.

Raymond moved to answer him, but upon opening his mouth the creature exploded outwards with a thick pollen-like cloud, which made its way into his mouth, eyes, and nose. Raymond began to sneeze and cough uncontrollably, rubbing at his eyes with the back of his hand. The creature sat entirely motionless as he did this, but the moment Raymond had recovered enough to cast a glance towards Bethany, he saw from the corner of his eye the creature dart towards her.

Micky, Bethany, and Raymond all immediately legged it, running back towards the counter with the intention of climbing on top of it, and joining Amanda in her safety. The creature without effort caught Raymond, but seemingly kept pace with him rather than overtaking. Despite the blur in his eyes and the sting in his throat from the strange pollen explosion, he attempted to push on faster and harder, trying in vain to outrun the small spider-crab-like monster. He rubbed at his eyes, managing to clear the blur from his left eye just in time to see the creature dart out from beside him, launch itself into the air, and slash Bethany's throat with one of its razor-sharp carapaced legs.

There was no hope nor attempt to save Bethany's life. A fountain of blood erupted, and her head fell backwards—only remaining connected to her torso by a thin slither of skin. She crumpled to the floor in silence, her blood puddled, and she was beyond the realm of medical assistance. It is doubtful that she would feel consoled by the fact that her death, and the creature's subsequent feeding on her corpse, had given the other three a chance to escape. Amanda, Micky, and Raymond did not waste the opportunity and sprinted the distance of the store, back down the aisles, locking themselves into the break room.

Within the break room they felt secure, or at least as secure as they could possibly feel within the store. None of the rooms were exactly airtight as, in a cheap attempt to air-condition the entire building with only one unit, neither the bathroom's nor the break room's walls went entirely to the ceiling. Even so, with hopes that the creature could not climb, they felt at the very least *safer* with a door between them.

"Oh god, oh Christ in a cupcake," bumbled Raymond.

"Screw your cupcakes!" responded Micky.

"It killed Bethany—oh my god, Bethany is dead," Amanda said awed.

"'Let's catch it, Micky. There could be a prize in it, Micky!'" Micky angrily quoted.

Raymond only moaned in response, a slow painful moan of agony.

"It killed Bethany," repeated Amanda, stunned.

Raymond continued to moan loudly.

Micky looked awkwardly away from Raymond as he continued to moan. The situation was bad, and two people were dead, and now he felt bad for his manager. In a strange way he hated Raymond for somehow making the situation about himself. Accidentally—while trying to avoid looking at Raymond, Micky made eye contact with Amanda, who seemed to have now somewhat composed herself. The two of them held a gaze for an awkward few seconds, and Raymond continued to groan.

Amanda darted her eyes from Micky to Raymond, and then back to Micky, then whispered, "Say something."

Micky did not want to play counsellor. He had his own problems to deal with, primarily the killer monster.

"Come on, say something. He must feel terrible; trying to catch it was his idea," she whispered.

"He should feel bad," Micky whispered back.

Raymond's anguished moans continued, and, after a pause, Amanda finally attempted to console Raymond herself:

"Raymond. Look, Raymond, it... it isn't *entirely* your fault," she tried.

"It sort of is," Micky cut in, which received an annoyed stare from Amanda, who despite thinking he may be right, didn't think such criticism at this time was helpful.

"*No*," she said forcefully, before relaxing her voice into more of a cooing.

"You were just doing what you thought was right," she soothed.

He groaned louder, then began to yell out in a painful cry.

"Come on, now; you can't blame yourself for a wild-animal attack," she reassured him.

"No... it's not that—well, it's that also, but..." he groaned further, "there's something wrong with my head," he cried.

"You're telling me," Micky commented, but then casting his mind back to the strange spore explosion began to wonder if Raymond hadn't received some kind of poisoning from it like Bethany had suggested they might. His eyes had begun to redden and he was perspiring heavily, and he continued to groan. Groan like the other man had.

"I... I think he might actually be really sick," Micky reluctantly admitted.

"He looks like he's in a lot of pain, yeah," agreed Amanda.

"Do you have Panadol?" Micky asked.

She didn't. Micky shifted uncomfortably, and Raymond moaned louder.

"I'm going to go to the medicine aisle and get some," Micky finally said with reluctance.

"You're crazy. That thing will kill you," Amanda objected, grabbing his arm.

"If we don't quiet him, it will hear us, come here, and do that anyway," he responded.

"Not if we just keep the door shut," she countered.

"You saw how fast it moves, and it jumps. Who's to say it can't climb? And if it can, it will just come over the top of the wall," reasoned Micky.

Amanda said nothing in response, but let go of his arm.

"I'll be quick," he assured her. "Just wait here with Raymond," he added.

"I'm not staying with him!" she hissed more harshly than she had intended, and then, drawing closer to Micky, added in a hushed whisper, "He's acting... like that guy that came in... I'm worried he'll... well, you know."

Micky *did* know, and nodded slowly.

"Fine, come, but we have to be fast and quiet," he replied, before turning to Raymond and offering, "Just hang in there, we'll be back in a moment."

Raymond groaned loudly, but not necessarily in response.

They made their way swiftly out of the break room, carefully shutting the door behind them, and moved towards the medicine aisle, scoring an unfortunate view of Bethany's corpse as they passed. She had had her abdomen torn open, and her organs and flesh were scattered about. Most of it was missing. From the corpse, bloody eight-legged footprints could be seen to wander off in zigzags. The footprints backtracked, retraced their steps, and then went off again.

"Look," Micky said, pointing out the random scatterings, "I think it's blind again," he postulated.

"It wasn't blind when it killed Bethany," Amanda hissed back.

"No, it wasn't," agreed Micky.

They quickly retrieved the pills as well as a handful of other items that they thought may prove useful. They then stealthily made their way back towards the break room but, upon clearing the final aisle before it, were disheartened to find the door standing open, and Raymond outside, slumped against the wall vomiting.

"Raymond, mate, you shouldn't be out here," Micky said, grabbing him and dragging him back into the small break room.

"I didn't... feel... so good," he slurred with drunken tongue.

"You don't look so good," Amanda agreed, handing him the Panadol and a bottle of water to wash it down.

Raymond accepted the items gratefully. His eyes were no longer red, but had instead dulled to a dark yellow, and his skin had become white and pasty. Beyond the acidic stench of vomit that could be smelt on his breath, there was also a dull background odour of rot slowly becoming discernable. Amanda was about to ask if the Panadol had helped, but before she had the chance she saw movement out of the corner of her eye, and ducked just in time to avoid the lunge of the creature, which evidently had entered the break room when the door had been left open.

Overshooting its target, the creature skidded, then quickly turned, and once more launched itself off the ground, this time in the direction of Micky who too only just dodged it. They burst out of the room, pulling Raymond along as best they could. The creature followed. Raymond staggered, tripped, and, proving too heavy for Micky and Amanda, fell, knocking himself unconscious on the tiled floor. The creature having launched itself from somewhere behind them, this time overshot all three, connected hard with a fixture, fell to the ground and darted off in its earlier zigzag motions, bumping into things as it went.

"It's blind again..." Micky commented more to himself than to Amanda. They each took an arm and dragged Raymond into the nearby bathroom, closing the door behind them.

Raymond's smell had worsened significantly, and—despite him occasionally twitching—a check of his pulse confirmed he was dead. There was a subtle noise, like the chattering of teeth, that emanated from his corpse.

"He's dead," Micky reported as calmly as he could.

"Dead also," Amanda commented.

"Yes," agreed Micky.

"That man dead, Bethany dead, Raymond dead," Amanda listed mechanically.

"What do we have?" Micky asked, trying to change the subject as best he could.

Amanda took stock of their supplies and in the same mechanical manner listed: "Panadol, one water bottle, some bandage wrap."

"Good," responded Micky, unsure what else he should say.

They then dragged Raymond's body into a toilet stall and were glad that its door went almost entirely to the floor. Only seconds after they had gotten him into the stall, the sickening nutshell crack could be heard, followed by a hiss, and the putrid odour of rotten meat could be smelt. Then they heard the scampering of small legs.

Micky pulled himself up to look over the stall door.

"What are you doing?!" hissed Amanda.

Micky didn't respond directly, instead commenting, "It is blind; this one can't see either!"

Amanda pulled herself up beside him and watched. It scampered around the cubicle, and even partially up the wall and door, but undeniably moved without purpose or direction.

"The other one was blind until it wasn't," warned Amanda cautiously, lowering herself back to the ground.

"The other one was blind until it was near Raymond, until he... well..." Micky trailed off.

"Died," finished Amanda.

"Yeah, that," agreed Micky.

He paused to gather his thoughts, then began again.

"I think they maybe see through the eyes of the infected, like, natural wi-fi or something; they use our eyes to see..." he offered awkwardly, expecting Amanda to shoot him down.

To Micky's surprise, she didn't.

In a horrific way it all made perfect sense to Amanda. The idea of a creature infecting another and using its senses wasn't that much more far-fetched in her mind than other things in nature she had heard of such as "hive minds", and "pack mentality", and she had always been a believer in extrasensory activity. Perhaps this was a creature that had evolved to enhance such things in those it infected, only to then take advantage of them.

"It was blind before it sprayed him with that pollen. That must be how it infects and spreads," she agreed.

"Well, neither of us had better get infected, then," Micky stated.

They sat on the floor of the bathroom beneath the sink and watched the stall doors. With the first creature still unaccounted for, and the second within the stalls, their place was only safe relative to the complete exposure of the store floor. Even then the creature had shown itself capable of launching great distances, and climbing, and so it was likely only a matter of time before this one either got out from the stalls, or the other got in from the store.

The odour of Raymond's corpse was of a spectacular stench, and on more than one occasion the creature scuttled up the back wall higher than the door height, and only through sheer luck redirected itself back into one of the three closed cubicles, rather than out into the general bathroom area. Amanda suggested they try relocating towards the break room, arguing that at least there was no creature within it, and reasoning that it would not be difficult to evade the remaining creature as, if their theory held true, it was currently blind. Micky instead suggested they make for the exit and try a proper escape, but was deterred from doing so when Amanda pointed out that the doors were locked, that the keys to open them were in the cubicle with Raymond, and that they had seen even more creatures outside.

Reluctantly Micky agreed with Amanda, and stood in order to make the attempt. He opened the bathroom door, and took a deep breath, preparing for the escape. His attempted calmness was, however, broken when, from behind them, the creature having finally managed to clear the cubicles, dropped to the floor with a loud *thwump*. There was now no time to delay. They had to get out of the confined space of the bathroom and into the break room once more. With Amanda close behind, Micky sprinted towards the break room and stepped through its doorway, only to place his foot directly down upon the hard outer shell of the first creature, which had evidently found its way within.

On connection, it spored him with a sick odour that invaded his eyes, nose and mouth. He grabbed Amanda's arm and, with his eyes closed, she ran him down the "chips & nuts" aisle. As he ran, Micky fumbled with his free hand to wrap the medical bandage over his eyes so that the creature would not be able to use them to see.

Before long the two of them were sat on the main counter, Micky blind, and Amanda watching as the two creatures randomly scuttled around the store.

The sun would rise soon, and the morning staff would start to arrive, but she knew they would be too late.

Outside, in the increased brightness, she could still see countless more creatures scampering about.

The stench of Bethany's blood mixed with the dull odour of rot permeating from Micky, and together they smelt of the crypt.

Occasionally Micky groaned and shuddered.

She had given him all the Panadol, but could tell the pain was still extreme.

She knew she shouldn't stay, but also knew that there was no escape.

Amanda had never really liked Micky. Heck, she had never really liked any of her co-workers but now, as it was just the two of them left, she felt almost a tribal need to be there. She felt that he shouldn't be left to die alone, just as surely as she felt she shouldn't be allowed to either.

The odour worsened, and Micky began to wail in pain.

The smell was spectacular, and Amanda could hear the strange chattering noise coming from within him.

He thrashed and he screamed and he chattered, and in his agony he clawed at his own face, and his skull, and his eyes, and in doing so he threw off the bandages that covered them.

The two of them, for a split second made eye contact. His eyes were dark and jaundice yellow. And Amanda heard a loud sickening crack, followed by a hiss.

A NEW DOG

Jacob's grandma had often spoken of the past, and was eventually taken away for it. She had painted it as a sort of utopia, in which things were plentiful, animals of all types were numerous, and man existed as one class without slaves or subordinates.

In her final days, she had spoken of other things.

The animals had been the first to go, she said. There was a great plague that had killed every non-human on the planet. With them gone, agriculture crumbled and a great famine unfolded. There was mass hysteria, violence, riots, and wars. Those few who remained fought over what little was left, firstly on a national level and then on a personal one. There was mass starvation, murder, and cannibalism.

These were all things Jacob's grandma had told him in harsh whispers and sporadic yells on her final days before they had taken her away, but as they wheeled her from the room she had whispered reassurances.

"Things *had* been good," she said. "There *was* love, and parties—and *food*, and equality—we didn't have labourers, those *slaves*, we didn't make *monsters*, and animals! We had animals, and dogs, *real* dogs," she had claimed.

It was distressing to see her in such a state, but Jacob's father (having called for the men to remove her), simply reassured him that she was sick, and that she would soon be fixed.

Jacob never saw his grandma again, and whenever he brought up the nightmares that she had described to him his father would quickly discredit them as the mad rambling of dementia, and whenever he spoke of the utopia she claimed they'd lost his father would discount these stories as mere nostalgia. Even so, Jacob often found it difficult on warm summer's days to not reminisce about those "days of plenty" in which he had never been permitted to live.

Mrs Haggardy loudly thwacked her ruler onto Jacob's desk, forcing him from his daydream, and drawing his eyes away from the warm day just outside the window. Those within the classroom—himself included—were not without some form of plenty. They were of the third generation of New Citizens—all of them children of government officials—and while their lives never quite matched the lofty descriptions his grandma had given, they at least never went hungry.

"Well?" she prompted. Her manner suggested there had been prior conversation that Jacob's inattentiveness had made him not privy to.

"What makes Man *Man*?" she prompted.

Jacob bristled. This, despite his inattentiveness, was a question he could answer, as New Philosophy was one of the subjects he had studied for the night before. Clearing his throat he thought back to his textbook and recited "Man is Man when he is, and behaves as such. A Man is a Citizen."

Mrs Haggardy smiled, straightened up, and reviewed the answer as "Very good", while walking back towards her blackboard's lesson markings.

Jacob always found these lessons awkward, and strangely unfulfilling. All New Philosophy was phrased in strange terminology such as this, and while he was aware that *Man* meant *Human* rather than *male*, he was still unsure what "Human is Human when he is, and behaves as such" could possibly mean. It was easy to give the answers found within the textbooks. They were short and pleasant enough to commit to memory, but repeating a phrase and knowing what it meant were two very different things, and despite often getting perfect grades he very rarely understood what it was that he supposedly knew.

"As Mr Collins has just said, an object can be defined when it looks in a way, and behaves in a manner, such as that which defines it." She looked out across the small classroom, paused on Mindy, a young freckled classmate, and prompted her for an example.

"A ball is a ball because it looks like a ball and bounces in a way such as a ball should, and a dog is a dog because it looks like a dog, and chases the ball," she proudly related the exact examples given from their textbooks to the approval of her teacher.

"Yes, excellent, and do you have one, Toby?" she asked a young brown-haired boy.

"A labourer is a labourer because it performs such tasks as a labourer must, and a Citizen is a Citizen because they are a productive member of Society, whose actions enhance—not detract from—the Culture. A Citizen has a soul," he proudly recited.

Mrs Haggardy congratulated his correct answer, then went on to exhaustively and mechanically list further such examples, but Jacob had already gone back to staring out the window and daydreaming in its summer glow. All it had taken was Mindy's mention of a dog, and the classroom and New Philosophy were all miles away.

Jacob had had a dog, and would have another one soon. His grandma had never liked it, and often referred to it in hurtful terms such as *perverse* and *ungodly*. On her saner days Jacob was able to learn that dogs in her day, just as labourers had been, were very different. Many things that she told him were confusing, as while words in Old Society were the same as words in New Society, they often meant entirely different things.

Dogs in Jacob's day now had to be specially ordered. They were expensive and hard to acquire, and his last dog, Spot, had become defective prematurely. It wasn't those last days, though, of Spot's defective behaviour, that Jacob now thought back to. He tried not to think of those days as best he could. The days of distant staring, long unnerving silences or the disturbing noises that broke those silences. He thought now not of that unpleasantness, but instead the earlier days of fetch in the park, and walks on the beach. Jacob didn't like to think of the last days, when the men from the company had come to take away his dog, just as they had his grandma.

Jacob was snapped back to the now by the sound of laughter. The children in the classroom were laughing, and it didn't take long for Jacob to become acutely aware that he was the subject of their amusement. He made his apologies, and requested the question to be repeated.

"What constitutes a soul?" Mrs Haggardy repeated with patient annoyance.

Theology and philosophy were one and the same in New Society, and gladdened that the subject was still one for which he had prepared, he recited from his previous night's readings once more:

"A soul is the collection of one's memories in purity and belongs to a Citizen," Jacob recited.

"Yes, good," she agreed again.

Jacob paused, and then raised his hand.

"Yes, Jacob?" the teacher prompted.

"But what does it *mean*?" he asked, to the giggle of a few students.

Mrs Haggardy returned to the board, picked up the chalk, and without writing anything turned back to the class.

"Our actions and experiences form memory, and our full collection of memory constitutes our selves. It is that 'self' devoid of flesh and form that is our soul," she elaborated.

Jacob pursed his lips with concern and Mrs Haggardy, noticing this, prompted him to speak if he had a further question.

"Is it just Citizens that have souls?" Jacob asked, after a brief pause.

Mrs Haggardy sighed. "It is defined as such, and so it is so," she responded bluntly.

"But don't labourers?" Jacob enquired, confused, and the eyes of his classmates widened at what could very well be interpreted as a purposeful contradiction of the teachings.

For a moment Mrs Haggardy too looked frustrated—or perhaps even flustered—but, after quickly composing herself she set to disputing the claim.

"No," she began, "they have only instinct, and only for that for which they have been trained and conditioned, but no memory. We teach a labourer to work, and perform all tasks required for the kind of labourer it is needed to be, but beyond that it retains no knowledge, and so there is no accumulation of memory, and so there is no soul. It knows nothing beyond that which it is trained and conditioned to know, and is therefore nothing more than it is. It behaves like a labourer and so it is not a Man, and it has no memory and so it cannot have a soul. Because it is not Man, and because it has no soul, it is not a Citizen. It is in these ways that a labourer behaves in a way such that is as themselves, and not of anything else."

"But if a labourer... or... *if those reconditioned do remember*—" began Jacob.

"There will be no further disturbances on this matter," ended Mrs Haggardy.

Jacob wasn't sure he understood... or perhaps he didn't agree with what his teacher told him about souls. He could remember his grandma having told him that "the eyes were the windows to the soul", and that "the soul was the spark you saw in someone's eyes". This had seemed reasonable when she had said it, but many things his grandma told him were, his parents informed him, incorrect. Despite this, looking around into the eyes of his classmates he could detect a spark of *something*—perhaps the soul—in each of them, and felt sure that on this matter his grandma must have been correct. But his classmates were all Man, and all Citizens, and so *should* have souls. But what of those who shouldn't? Had no labourers ever had a soul, had no dogs? On this matter he remained unconvinced.

Another question occurred to Jacob, and so he raised his hand again. "Is it wrong that we make things into that which they previously were not?" he asked.

Mrs Haggardy paused her pacing. "New Morality is next week," she stated shortly.

Jacob remained clearly uncomfortable and so, sighing heavily, the teacher relented and agreed to address the next week's lesson plans early.

"Wrongness is an action against the Society, and Society is made up of Citizens," she began.

"As we covered earlier, 'a Citizen is a Citizen because they are a productive member of Society, whose actions enhance—not detract from—the Culture. A Citizen has a soul.' There are many who are less fortunate than you, who fail to meet this first criterion, and so lose their right to the second. There are those who are not as wealthy and educated, and who have little or no individual future prospects."

She continued, "If one is in extreme debt to Society, but lives desolate and with no hope of repaying that debt, then they are detractors from our Culture, and so are not Citizens. If one is a criminal then they are against Society, and so are not Citizens. In the cases of the desolate, they live in poverty, hunger, and starvation. It would be wrong for us to continue to allow their suffering, and so they are relieved of their souls and from such societal burdens only fit for Man, and are repurposed in a way in which they may be of at least some benefit to Society. The reconditioning and the retraining are always very thorough and, with no memory of what they were, they are free, and even *happy* to be that which they have become," she finished.

Jacob pondered what she had said. It seemed wrong to him, but he wasn't entirely sure how. If someone wasn't able to remember what they had been, he supposed it wouldn't matter to them what they had become. And, as she had mentioned, those who were reconditioned were previously living in poverty, and surely living a life of ignorance as a well-fed labourer was less cruel than allowing someone to continue living as a fully aware poverty-stricken desolate? Even so, Jacob doubted that he himself, *burdened by his own memories*, would choose to be remade rather than to suffer. But, were he not to have his memories, would he miss them? He enjoyed being Man, but that was from the perspective of someone who *was* Man, and *did* have a soul and *was* a

Citizen. It would be wrong of him to not want to be Man, or to not behave in a manner such as Man does, seeing as he was one, just as it would be wrong for a labourer not to want to be a labourer and a—"

"Do you understand, Jacob?" Mrs Haggardy prompted again, interrupting his thoughts.

"Yes," Jacob responded automatically, though with more conviction than he actually felt.

Jacob thought back to his dog. He wasn't really sure he agreed that only Citizens had memory, and only Citizens had souls. Couldn't it be possible for a labourer—*despite its retraining and reconditioning*—to remember that which it once was, or develop an understanding of that which it had become? Wasn't it possible for a dog to have a soul?

Spot had lacked that look in its eyes—that soulful look— that he could see in all the children around him. Or at least Spot had lacked that look *for most of the time* Jacob had had it. Jacob's mind turned again to those final days with Spot— the days he tried his best to forget, and the day when the men had come to take his dog away. On those days Spot had had a soulful look, but it was not the bright spark of Jacob's classmates, but a dim sort of shine that was sad and made Jacob feel guilty, and dirty... and then there were those *noises*.

The classroom lesson had moved on, but Jacob interrupted it by raising his hand, and brought back the earlier abandoned subject once more, demanding: "But what about when they *do* remember?!"

Mrs Haggardy gave him a stern look. "The reconditioning and retraining process is *very* thorough. It is very rare, *almost unheard of*, for those converted—a labourer or *what have you*—to remember anything from before they became that which they are, and when they do it is taken care of."

Rare.

Almost unheard of.

But not non-existent.

Jacob *knew* with growing certainty that despite what his teacher said, in Spot's eyes he had seen a soul, but it was one that was battered, tortured and fearful. And he knew for a fact that dogs, some dogs, *could* remember.

Was it wrong for his dog to have displayed these traits and to have exhibited that which it had no business in showing, or was it wrong that a creature that so evidently had a soul was not considered a Citizen?

Jacob wasn't sure, but these questions had been growing and festering inside of him ever since those final days. Jacob now couldn't help but think of then, and of those noises that he had heard Spot make while the men had prepared to wheel his dog away. Noises that Jacob wished he could forget, but felt certain he never would.

They were wheezes, they were whispers and, to Jacob's astonishment, *they were words.*

Words that were rasped and drawn out and painful, but words undeniably.

Words that were a name—*Billy*—said over and over again.

It whispered and Jacob's father held him back, and quietly assured him that his next dog would be better behaved, and Spot continued to whisper *Billy, Billy, Billlllly,* repeated over and over again in pain and in sorrow.

Disturbed by the sounds made by the creature, Jacob had broken free from his father and screamed, "Who's Billy?!"

—and in agony and in anguish it had answered, "I was."

THE WALK HOME

Michael awoke, sat up—just partially—and bumped his head hard. It was dark and, as he was usually a heavy sleeper, he was not accustomed to waking while the sun was not yet out. The air smelt musty, damp, earthy and thin. Deep breaths failed to relieve his lungs and, as if he were atop a mountain, Michael could not help but feel endlessly deprived of oxygen.

This was an awakening for Michael unlike any other; this was an awakening in which Michael had been buried alive.

There was a part of him that vaguely knew of his situation the moment he had bumped his head against the coffin's lid—or perhaps even before he had sat up. This knowledge was, however, not entirely conscious. Instead it was revealed to him by that quiet voice that whispers often ignored and unseen truths—deduced by the subconscious—and often mistaken as premonition. It was the voice of insight that, without apparent evidence, would correctly conclude from the minutest clues everything from spousal cheating to the coming rains, and deliver its discoveries in the form of unease and discomfort. However, aided by the smell, the cramped space, the shortage of air, and the darkness, it did not take long for Michael's conscious to catch up with the horrid truth of his subconscious' insight. Within moments he quite rightly reasoned out his predicament, and it panged at him as the ultimate rejection.

Michael knew that he was not the first person to have been buried alive. As a boy he could recall having heard schoolyard tales of live burials having taken place. He distinctly remembered stories of bells being tied to toes, so that, in the event of such unfortunate happenings, those wrongly suspected of being a corpse could simply wriggle their foot to alert those above of their premature interments. These cases, as he understood them, had, however, been in antiquity. Occurrences such as these were of a domain before medical science broke from natural philosophy to become a true discipline in its own right; in this day of technological marvels, what possible excuse could there be for the likes of him—*or anyone*—to find themselves in such a situation? In all his adult life Michael could recall no such incidents as this as having ever occurred.

Wriggling his own toes, Michael noted that he himself had no such string. There would be no bell to tell of his predicament. Michael began to recall other, less pleasant, stories of those who, like him, had been buried without a bell mechanism. Stories of bodies exhumed decades too late, their coffins revealing scratch marks and embedded fingernails. The jaws of their premature occupants' skulls twisted in horrified screams unheard. Memory and imagery flow more freely in the lonely dark, and these tales quickened Michael's breath and heartbeat, and ate away at the already depleted oxygen. Michael would have to combat his panic with forced calmness and reflection, were he to avoid perishing in the dark damp.

He took a breath and held it. It *was* dark, and it *was* damp, and Michael slowly began to fathom just how wet his surroundings were. From above him soft muddy droplets dripped periodically onto his cheek. It had been a cold autumn, and it had been a wet autumn, and evidently, it was or had been raining. Despite Michael's shortness of breath giving evidence that both the coffin and hole in which he was buried were fairly airtight, waterproof it evidently was not. Now fully awake and entirely free of grogginess, Michael noted that he lay in what was roughly half an inch of muddied water, within which he could feel the movements of soil-dwelling creatures as they curled and wriggled around him.

But why was he here? There were ways to tell whether someone was dead, *weren't there*? This had happened before, in the Dark Ages, but *this* was the twenty-first century. Sure, people would fall into comas, or find themselves deeply unconscious, but these days one shouldn't be buried unless they were dead, and they shouldn't be considered dead unless a doctor was entirely certain of the matter.

He had, of course, been sick.

This could be said to be true for most of Michael's adult life. He had, amongst other things, a weak heart, under-performing kidneys, dizzy spells, poor eyesight, and flat feet to boot! And... as of late his health *had* gotten worse... *somehow*...

Michael tried to concentrate through a pounding headache. *A lack of oxygen can cause headaches and lethargy.* He shook his head to try and clear such negativity, but in doing so only made himself more light-headed and dizzy. He couldn't quite remember *how* he had gotten worse, or even *when* he had gotten worse, but despite this gap in recollection two things were abundantly clear. Firstly, that he had, *at some point*, gotten bad enough that some crackpot quack had declared him dead, and secondly, that he would need to free himself of his new home soon, lest he suffocate from lack of oxygen, or drown in the rising pool of mud and worms.

Through careful minimalistic manoeuvring Michael was able to reposition his hands from down by his sides to in front of his face and, by lightly tapping on the lid of his oppressive confines, he was relieved to learn that his wife had indeed gotten him as cheap a coffin as his will had stipulated. She had seen him buried, not in an expensive casket of well-fitted materials (as she herself thought proper), but instead a coffin constructed cheaply of wooden planks and nails—barely a crate in design.

It was from no other motive when requesting such burial methods than a want for financial frugality, and a desire to avoid post-mortem ostentation that had led Michael to choosing such a cheap final resting place. Regardless of reason, however, the thin wooden planks of his surroundings gave him a chance, *though marginal*, of escape. He ran his fingers along the planks where they joined imperfectly, and felt as he did so the dirt and mud disturbed by his actions fall through the cracks, dropping like cold raindrops onto his face and chest. For a second he felt a ping of regret for not having asked to be buried shallow, but then found himself merely grateful to not have opted for cremation. The situation, while dire, was not hopeless.

On a dry day any escape from his grave would likely be impossible. Despite the cheapness of his coffin, it was brand new, and it would be unlikely to yield to any pressure he could possibly muster. These were however, fortunately, *not* the optimal conditions designed for the coffin. With the added weight and strain from the rain and dampened soil there was a chance, however slim, that he could cause the wooden planks that surrounded him to buckle and break. Pounding his fists upwards with as much force as he could muster within such close proximity, Michael began to hit upon his coffin's lid, attempting to cause it to cave in upon him.

At first, it was slow work. With each pound it seemed that the planks, and certainly the dirt (excluding the small clumps that fell through the cracks), gave no ground. This changed, however, quite suddenly. Through the shifting weight of his hits and the increased weight of the soaked soil, the planks gave, and the earth collapsed inwards.

It was reflex, and reflex alone, that allowed Michael to inhale deeply—consuming what little was left of his oxygen—just as the dirt cut off any hope for further relief. The weight was crushing, and the wooden planks dug painfully into his legs and abdomen, driven in like nails by the pressure above. Human nature left Michael, and was replaced by animalistic terror. Thus it was not the civility of man but survival instinct—pure and bestial—that drove him to claw, wriggle, and writhe his way upwards towards the surface.

Michael moved like a worm through the damp soil. Were it not for the rain he could never have made it farther than the collapsed coffin, but so malleable had the land become that he swam as much as he crawled. Through mud-like water, and through terror and encroaching darkness, he swam as the black mud of the grave slid down his throat and attacked his lungs with a painful growing pressure. The mud drove the threat of suffocation through his mind with a dull thudding thunder that his ears echoed as his pulse raced, then slowed despite his adrenaline and building fear. Michael found himself deafened by the silent echoes screamed from the deepest recesses of forgotten space.

Michael had been sick.

There was no moon tonight, only blackness, and he had been sick. He remembered his sickness as he lay flat on his back beside his own open grave.

He had no recollection of having made it through the last few feet of earth. That journey had been made by the same subconscious controls that had first noted his peril. It was still raining, and the drops fell down upon him heavily, washing the dirt and the worms and the maggots from his flesh, so that they pooled in the small puddle that marked the indentation of his collapsed coffin.

Here rests Michael Andrews his headstone claimed, and with effort he struggled to his feet, intent on making a liar out of his own grave marker.

Standing and limping, Michael made his way painfully through the blackness, past several other similarly pooling graves along the soaked mud and neglected path, and out through the iron gates of the hillside cemetery. He was not the only one to have found his way out this evening, and yet they all walked alone.

It occurred to Michael through vague and distant memory that this was the first time in some while that he had walked at all. Before the coffin, and before the burial, he had been sick. *Really sick.* Bedridden with some kind of flu or virus of the blood. Weakened, drowsy—"dying" Michael remembered his doctor having assessed, as he reached the porch of his family home and rapped upon the door.

In the rain Michael found his memories flowed freely. He remembered clearly now, *almost obviously*, that he *had been dying.*

Not only that, but he could even remember having died.

Strange.

The door swung open, suddenly breaking Michael from his thoughts as the image of his wife appeared before him.

Immediately, he was sickened.

His wife, once so lovely to him, appeared now poisonously tainted by the flair of life. Her skin (though paled slightly by fear) was pinkish white and held to her flesh in a disgusting display of youth and vitality. It showed no wrinkle nor blemish. Her widened eyes shone bright blue and clear white. Her red lips were uncracked and unpeeled. She smelt of fresh perfume and summer days, and she began to scream.

Michael took a half-step back, repulsed by what he saw, but entirely unsure why it disgusted him so. He couldn't understand what she was screaming at either. She was, he supposed, justified in her surprise, seeing that he was supposed to be dead, but before he could finish reasoning out such things, she fainted, and Michael was forced to catch her and ease her to the floor.

Her skin was warm to the touch, and Michael drew back in disgust, still unsure of what it was that disgusted him so. She repulsed him but as he stared at her he could not fathom why. She was seemingly—*objectively*—no different to when last he had seen her.

He stood and saw the hallway mirror, previously obscured by his fainted wife.

She had not changed. And she had been right to scream.

Staring back at Michael was a reflection—*his own reflection*—though he did not immediately recognise it. He was lit by the porch light, which cut through the night and revealed rotten flesh, peeled away to show bone. Maggot infested. Crawling with worms. Dark grey, and white with mould.

His was the visage of the damned, the dead, the forgotten, and the beyond.

Stirring, his wife murmured quiet nonsense, and even in her semiconscious state emitted an aura of life now hateful to Michael. A vitality which invoked within him bile and sick. She had become to him the other, and to look upon her was to poison in him her memory. She had become as lost to him as he had to her.

Limping and dragging his way back towards the cemetery, Michael clawed at the damp earth and did his best to return to his home. The flesh from his hands and the nails from his fingers gave more easily than the dirt he clawed, and as he dug he soon saw bone and tendon.

Around him Michael saw that others too had begun to return.

Some sobbed, and some whispered of what they had seen, but all dug towards their graves.

CALL OF THE VOID

Charles lay on his side in the lumpy sweat-stained bed of his apartment.

Eyes open. Awoken by a buzz from without that was more often a hum from within. His head pounded, and he had the sweats. Charles was hungover. He was—he quickly assessed—*extremely* hungover.

Charles's head pounded from the booze, though it usually hummed, and the hum from within was now replaced by a buzz from beyond. As per normal, his bedroom was overly warm—the air conditioner had never worked, and the landlord had never cared. In summer the apartment was prone to bugs, spiders, and flies. They came through the windows that could not seal tightly, under the draughty doors, and through the cracks in the walls that led into other apartments.

The bedroom was overly warm, the apartment was overly musty, the carpet had mould, and Charles had a hangover.

Charles could not remember how he had gotten home.

Being in his home without remembering how he had gotten there was a fascinating and somewhat terrifying oddity. Charles didn't drink anymore. It had been *years* since Charles had even touched a drop, let alone allowed himself to become blackout drunk. Despite this, blackout drunk was something Charles had evidently gotten. How his night had ended was a mystery veiled in the darkness of total inebriation. He wasn't one to trust himself drunk—he wasn't even one to trust himself sober—and what antics he may have gotten up to when in the autopilot state of his worst vices worried him greatly.

Closing his eyes tightly, Charles attempted to reconstruct how the night had progressed, and how the day preceding it had begun. With effort he forced his thoughts past the pounding headache and the strange buzzing. His memories were disordered. Yesterday could have easily been childhood, and childhood could have easily been yesterday. Charles sometimes felt himself a time traveller, capable of seamlessly placing himself (mentally) back in time to re-experience his own memories exactly as though they were initially unfolding. However, with the headache and the buzzing he found that today his thoughts disobeyed him. They took him to wherever in time they pleased. They jumbled, fought for primacy, and were given free range within his muddled mind.

Charles was five. There hadn't been a buzz then—that had only come this morning—but he had always hummed. In childhood Charles assumed that all children hummed. He had no frame of reference, so how was he to know that an ever-present hum that urged and inspired was an abnormality? Children only know what they are told, and in the same way that he had never questioned why it was that he became tired towards the end of the day, he had never questioned why there was a hum. It was a dull vibration that compelled him to action. Action that would often lead to trouble. It urged him to draw on walls, and insisted that he pull on girls' hair, but was never anything that Charles had ever given much thought to. The hum—so far as Charles was aware—simply was.

The room smelt of mould and sweat and filth, and amongst the odours that usually assaulted him upon awakening within his run-down firetrap of an apartment was another scent that he could not place. It was one that he had smelt before, though he was unsure of where or when. His mind tried in vain to place it, dancing over various experiences from camping to driving to fishing. He was in a coffee house, and he was at a funeral. Once a rat had died in the wall of his apartment, and when told of it his landlord had simply said that "the smell would pass in time". The room vibrated with the buzz from beyond, and his head pounded. The smell did not matter—it was just another addition to his already unpleasant state of living, and so, redirecting his mind back to the task at hand, Charles attempted to remember what had unfolded the night before.

Charles was twenty, and it was yesterday. It had been 8 am Sunday morning when he had pushed his way through the paint-peeled door of his apartment, and made his way down the dreary hallway towards the elevator. The small rusted number on his door claimed that he lived in Apartment 2, but this was only because the seven that once preceded the two had long since fallen off. The elevator began to move, and Charles swallowed the last of his breakfast (a piece of toast) as he descended the seven floors to ground level. Church wouldn't start until 9 am, and it was only a fifteen-minute walk from his apartment, but Charles always aimed to get there early. He enjoyed the social aspects of the congregation that took place before church, and usually tried to arrive early enough to talk with others before morning mass. As he made his way to church the hum of his mind had mixed with that of the traffic, but the recollection of both remembered sounds now struggled against the reality of his pounding headache and the unusual buzz. The room was hot, sticky, and noisy, and it was only through much mental effort that Charles was capable of conjuring forth his recollections. He struggled to maintain focus on just one as they skipped and jumbled through his mind.

Charles was seven, and a friend had just informed him of an imaginary companion named "Mr Beatles". Mr Beatles was a large purple giraffe with whom his friend claimed to have gone on many adventures. Then, just as now, the ever-present humming within Charles's mind had no such physical appearance as Mr Beatles was claimed to have. Charles's humming also had neither voice nor personality. When the hum spoke to Charles it did not do so through any means of communication that he fully understood, but instead through compulsions that, much like hunger or the need to go to the bathroom, he either felt he couldn't, or shouldn't, ignore. These compulsions appeared within his mind but felt as though they were not his own. They were, he felt, completely alien. Charles did not understand why his imaginary friend was so different and less describable than that of the other children's, but found himself comforted and normalised to know that he was not the only one who felt a presence that compelled him.

Charles rolled onto his back and stared blankly at the ceiling. There was a stain above his bed that he could never quite explain. It appeared to be damp—always damp—but his apartment was not the top floor, and so what it was damp with Charles was completely uncertain. When he had first noticed the stain he had worried that the apartment above had left their tap on, and half expected the stain to continue to grow, sag the ceiling, and then finally collapse in on him. It never did grow any larger, nor did it ever dry. Pointing a torch directly at the stain made it glisten like a rainbow, revealing that it—*whatever it was*—was more grease than water. The landlord, when asked to investigate, repeatedly claimed that there was no such stain and had gone so far as to deny its existence even as Charles stood with his finger pressed into its soggy, greasy dampness. Now, as Charles attempted once more to refocus his mind to the events of yesterday, he found himself staring into the shiny stain and wondering—not for the first time—if it were truly there.

Charles was once again back in front of the parkland church, and it was once again Sunday. He claimed that he always gets there early because he enjoys the company of the congregation. He has even often repeated this lie to himself. In truth, there was only one for whom his efforts were made, in an attempt to see her. She was sitting there on the bench outside the church as he had approached yesterday morning. She was sitting on the park bench, and as the cool Sunday breeze blew through her hair—framed by the impressive masonry of the old building—she looked as though she was an angel. In a strange way Charles saw both her and the church as one and the same, and felt them both to be equally his saviour. It was only during church, and it was only while talking to Mandy, that his hum completely receded. No compulsion drove him during either of these two forms of worship, and it was only in these moments that he ever felt himself truly content. On that Sunday, yesterday morning, they had made small talk while they waited for the large wooden doors to open. She had laughed when she was supposed to, and where his practice of their conversations had assured him she would. The doors had opened and their conversation had been cut off. The humming returned and under its compulsion Charles had asked Mandy to lunch. He had done so just as though it were no big deal, and as if he hadn't before pained himself over the thought of doing so, but never followed through.

The hum was a compulsion that drove him further and harder than he could ever drive himself. Sometimes he called it his courage, though he knew such a label was dishonest. Courage was when you faced something despite its known adversity, but his compulsions were too often the creator of the adversities he faced. The hum had compelled

Charles to ask Mandy to lunch that morning, just as the buzz from beyond now drove him to sit up in bed.

Charles was thirteen, dismayed, and alone. Making friends never appeared to be as easy as keeping them, and as he entered high school all friendships he had formed in his younger years declined and dissipated. It was with increasing resignation that Charles found he had difficulties relating to the other children. Not least of his concerns was his discovery of their apparent abandonment of the notion of imaginary friends. They claimed proudly to have "grown out of them", and mocked Charles for being slow to do so. This was a further frustration as he had only deceitfully claimed in the first place that his compulsions had personality and form in order to fit in with theirs, and now, having maintained the claim, was mocked for it. In these years his humming grew louder, and was increasingly difficult to deny. At age fifteen, when finally Charles felt himself entirely unable to ignore his compulsions, it was only fortuitous that he had already begun to be seen by staff members of the school as a constant target of bullying.

The boy that Charles had taken to with a hammer in shop class had, in actuality, never once harassed Charles and was only the unfortunate target of his compulsions when finally the humming had grown far too loud, and far too violent. In truth, Charles liked the boy, but knew all too well the troubles that would come if he said so. Taking a hammer to someone you liked, unprovoked, was just something that normal people didn't do. Charles knew this, but what could he do? He was already extremely unpopular; the other boys hated him, and the girls feared him. If he had admitted that the boy he hit had never bullied him, and that the attack was entirely unprovoked, it would raise too many questions. They would ask him why. They would learn about his hum. They would force him to see a doctor—the white-coat "funny farm" variety—and he would be further ostracised, slapped with the label of some kind of embarrassing medical oddity, called "mad" and "nuts", and then no-one would ever be his friend. Fearing such things, Charles made sure to agree with all that the teachers said of him and his victim. He agreed that he had been the subject of the boy's harassment for far too long, that name calling had turned physical, and that (being the smaller of the pair) Charles had grabbed for the hammer to defend himself.

"Don't take what he did too personally," one teacher had told Charles. "The boy just has no conscience."

This was the first time Charles had heard the word and, asking what it meant, was relieved to learn that it referred to "that little voice in your head that guides you". Charles immediately became convinced that this "conscience" was merely an adult-friendly rebranding of the "imaginary friend". While he still wasn't sure why his "little voice" never spoke to him in words, he was relieved once more that it was not just he who felt a presence within him, though he found it curious and alarming that only his appeared to drive him towards violence.

In the wall of the sticky smelly bug-ridden apartment in which Charles now sat, there was a small fist-sized hole that he had punched three years earlier. He had done this for no other reason than that he had been compelled to do so, and that he knew the compulsion would not stop until he did. He had been seventeen at the time and, having just moved into the apartment, feared that the damage would immediately result in his being evicted. Fortunately, when next his landlord came by for an inspection, the hole in the wall was not noticed as distinct beyond any of the apartment's already existing inadequacies. There was, poking through this hole, a thin layer of insulation, which the landlord insisted was not asbestos.

"You should count yourself lucky the place even has insulation," he had said. "Most places don't, you know?" he had gone on to claim.

The hammer and the fist were by no means isolated incidents. The hum more often than not compelled Charles to violence or self-destructive tendencies. He had, while reading *Reader's Digest*, learned of the term *l'appel du vide*, or "the call of the void", a fairly common phenomenon where, when standing on a high ledge or driving against oncoming traffic, many people feel a brief urge to jump or to turn into said traffic. It was this common phenomenon that Charles had then attempted to convince himself was what he experienced on an almost constant basis. This term suited Charles well in his quest for self-normalisation, and it allowed him to continue to justify never seeking psychological help.

Since the incident with the hammer, Charles had experimented with different ways of ignoring or drowning out the hum. There had been meditation, heavy exercise, loud music, and self-medication. The latter he had depended on the most and, having landed him in hospital twice, it had been the most disastrous. In small doses alcohol and drugs had managed to dull the hum, but he was never able to limit himself to small doses. During the inevitable large doses it was his conscious mind that took the back seat and the hum that was given full rein, and when the hum was given full rein, terrible things would follow.

Charles had not had a drink now for two years—not since the bar fight that had seen him sent to Alcoholics Anonymous—which had encouraged church. That is to say, he had not had a drink for two years until, apparently, last night.

Had it been at the lunch with Mandy that he had had a drink?

Or was it afterwards that he drank, either celebrating the lunch, or trying to forget its failure?

Charles pushed his knuckles into his eyes and tried to drown out the pounding headache that filled his head and the buzzing that filled the room.

Charles was twenty, and he had just left church with Mandy.

Charles was always good at hiding his compulsions around Mandy. Mandy did not know of his past, and when she asked him he told lies and half-truths, figuring that to do so was okay just so long as he himself remained genuine. Lunch had become coffee, and coffee had become dinner, and their Sunday following church had taken them from a deli to a cafe to a restaurant to a bar. Charles had drunk, and became drunk, because Mandy had asked him if he drank, and he couldn't think of an excuse to tell her as to why he didn't. As liquor was consumed, his ever-present hum faded into the dullness of his inebriation, and the lines between his own actions and those he was compelled towards were blurred. Despite his usually photographic memory, Charles's recollection of this time became stilted and fragmented. Three lines of conversation could be called up to recollect entire hours, and locations became confusingly interchangeable. He could remember dancing, laughing, and briefly being concerned that Mandy would judge him for his small, grease-stained, bug-ridden apartment. Somewhere between 1 and 2 am Charles's memory ceased entirely—annoyingly during the pleasant recollection of kissing Mandy.

Following this moment of total blackout there was nothing more than a void in time, then his awakening to the pounding of his headache, the uncertainty of the night before, and his usual hum from within, replaced by the strange buzz from beyond. It was late in the morning and Charles was back in the present once more, in the overly warm dimness of his small bedroom.

It had been hours since Charles had first begun to attempt his recollection of the day prior, and hours more before the thudding in his head dulled, and the familiar hum returned. The hum was within, and yet the buzz he took to be of the same origin remained beyond.

They vibrated in uneasy unison, the hum within, and the buzz beyond.

Charles was compelled out of bed—a bed which he had slept in alone. He now noted this with some significance as he moved from under the grease-stained ceiling, past the small asbestos hole and towards his bedroom door. It was— he realised with dull confusion—within his own apartment that the memory of he and Mandy kissing had taken place. Where then was she now, he wondered, and had they parted on good terms?

As the hum drove him towards the door, the buzzing grew in intensity and, standing at its precipice, Charles felt certain that the door itself was the source of the outer vibrations. Vibrations that, Charles now realised with a cold sweat, were doubtlessly beyond. A noise that existed outside his own mind and head, that existed with true form, independent of him. Charles half expected, when taking the doorknob in hand, for it to rattle about wildly, and was shocked to find it entirely inanimate, and yet the buzzing grew louder.

It increased, and grew with further intensity.

The buzz from beyond the door. The buzz that vibrated with neither compulsion nor desire, and yet buzzed all the same. Without want or urging, Charles swallowed deeply, and turned the handle—*Is this courage?*—and pushed on through.

Numbness.

Charles's hum had grown silent—or was simply drowned out—as the buzzing confirmed itself not to be the product of his own mind, but the scream of the black swarm.

The buzzing—the wing beat of the uncountable masses—which moved with hellish speeds, and were the storm clouds of man's darkest days.

The apartment was warm, sticky, and humid. The air-conditioning had never worked and in summer the apartment was prone to bugs, spiders, and flies.

Flies that had now returned en masse, swarming, crawling, and wriggling their way inside, through the windows that could not seal tightly, under the draughty doors, or through the cracks in the walls that led into other apartments.

In countless numbers they had congregated, and in their black mass they swarmed the brutalised remains of his saviour Mandy, in the dim unpleasant apartment and the warmth of the late Monday morning.

THE TREE THAT BIRTHED HIM

The stars shone brightly, just as they had two nights prior on the evening Larry Carol had been born. Things had been different then. Then he had had the comfortable certainty of conviction that comes with youth. Now, as he stood staring at the tree that birthed him, he reflected on how things had grown far more complicated.

Choice had never come into it. Larry hadn't chosen to be born—no-one does—and had he known what it would entail he surely would have chosen to remain safely non-existent. But Larry had never been given that option, and so here he stood.

He had been nothing, and then there was a brief struggle for life, and now he was... *was what?*

He was Larry Carol.

Or was he?

There was no-one now more qualified to be Larry Carol than he, and there was no-one he was more like than Larry. The only person he had met had had no doubt in their mind that he was Larry, and he was, in almost every way (barring some slight biological and neurological differences), completely identical to what Larry had been. It is unlikely any detective would suspect or condemn him as an imposter. He had the memory, he had the body, and he had the cadence of Larry. There were, of course, small differences in the mind—mainly experiences that he had but that Larry had lacked. Experiences that made him the latest link in a chain that extended beyond history. Experiences and knowledge about what he was that Larry wasn't. This knowledge imposed itself on him with great significance. It was the hauntingly devastating awareness that he was, in fact, not Larry Carol.

Larry Carol was dead.

On Thursday the 30th of April, Larry Carol—having discovered a strange tree growing in his backyard and touched it—was paralysed, covered in sap, and then digested. The sap had then hardened, hollowed, filled with nutrients, and then, on Friday the 1st of May, it had cracked and given birth to... Larry Carol—not the Larry Carol who had died, but this new creature who, beyond being anything else, *was* Larry Carol.

It is fortunate that Larry had been born on the weekend. It takes time to fully comprehend the knowledge extracted through the pupal stage of development, and never before had his line encountered and digested a creature of such complexity as Larry had been. His line had never before incorporated—and so was not accustomed to—things such as language, clothes, cars, and coffee breaks, let alone the concept of work. It was a staggering amount of information and nuance to take in that seemingly dwarfed the full ancestral memory accumulated throughout a long history of replicative assimilation and reproduction. For the first time in his line's long history Larry found himself contemplating just how terrible a task it was for his species to perform mimicry on any creature that it ensnared.

Was mimicry the correct word?

There were more subtleties to how this human species perceives the world than he was accustomed to, and this was becoming ever more apparent with every passing moment. Mimicry, he fathomed, implied imitation, and in many senses went hand in hand with mockery. Was he a mockery of what Larry had been? Was he a mere mimic of the man he had digested? A mockery was usually considered as less than what was being mocked. Was he—as the latest link in his line—less than the creature he had digested, or had he—by adding Larry to his line—become more than either his line or Larry had ever been?

Larry tried out the word *copy*; in his mind it felt more accurate than *mimic*, but something inside him whispered other, crueller, suggestions. Suggestions like *perversion*, and *abomination*.

That voice, too, was new to Larry's line, as were most nuances that made up the human experience.

He could recall all previous beings that had been brought into his line. His was a branch that led back to the first of his species. When he reproduced—which, judging by the welling inside him, he soon would—his consciousness would end, but all those who branched from him would recall it as their own, just as he could recall all who had led to him. In turn, those who branched from them would spawn dozens more branches themselves, and his experience would be propagated through all of them, across the planet, the galaxy, and time itself. All who branched from and followed him would know his line and his experience, but he himself would end, and this was the first time any being in his line (and, so far as he was aware, his species) had ever been aware of and felt troubled by this knowledge.

The real Larry Carol was *dead*. Dead in the very real, very normal human usage of the term. Dead. The word echoed through the head of his copy. *Dead, gone, deceased, no more.* There was no continuity for the former Larry Carol. He had had a consciousness and that consciousness had now ended. He had undergone a reverse birth, and now he no longer existed. His replacement felt keenly that the original would have found no solace in knowing that another creature with his exact memory and knowledge now existed. He felt this because, deep down, he knew that he too would find no solace in those who branched from him continuing from his own non-existence. For the first time in his line's long history of experience he mourned, both for the one he had digested, and for what end would inevitably come for him.

Why should he feel like this? His line had absorbed and copied countless living creatures before. They were all a part of him—he could recall their existence millennia ago with the same ease that he could recall Larry's last weekend. He could recall having been on countless planets, asteroids, and in space itself. His line predated even the first creature absorbed into it to have had the concept and sense of time. But in all the eons that his ancestral memory stretched back, they had never felt... what?

Regret? Compassion? Love?

These were all symptoms of a greater problem. When on Saturday the 2nd of May a female of the species—Larry's girlfriend—had come over, he had felt a love for her. None in his line had experienced such a thing before. It was a strong caring for what she had been to Larry, and what she now was to him. While she was there he had pretended that all that he was was Larry, and that his experience did not go beyond Larry's, and it was wonderful, and when she left it was greatly disturbing.

He had never had to pretend to be a spouse before... he did not even think he needed to do so now. It didn't benefit the furtherance of his species in any way that he could think of. A *partner* (in the human sense of the word) was not necessary for his spawning. His way was to diminish into spores, which would propagate into lifetrees that would digest and copy those who came into contact with them, resulting in branches and further lines. It didn't fully matter what creature was to be digested—a bird could just as easily have been ensnared by the lifetree that had birthed him as Larry had been. There would be no specific benefit drawn from Larry's girlfriend being digested. So why had he bothered to spend time with this human creature with whom he himself had never interacted? The answer was simple yet baffling. To be around her had felt... *nice.*

Love and *compassion* were something no previous chain in his line would have been able to contextualise. They hadn't even had an awareness of self to any true degree, and instead existed on animalistic tendencies. The other ancestral links that predated him had been akin to a bug, a worm, a spider, a crustacean, a rodent—they had never been those exactly, but they were the closest equivalents within Larry's understanding.

And therein lay the problem.

Larry's understanding—the ability to contextualise thought, feeling, individuality—these were Larry's domain. These were experiences and comprehensions to which none who made up his line had ever before been exposed. Until Larry, his line had not had to deal with self-awareness.

His evolutionary priority was to reproduce, but before Larry he didn't understand the concept of evolutionary theory, he just performed it.

Without knowledge or self-awareness his species absorbed, mimicked, and reproduced. There was that word again, *mimic*, but perhaps it was true; perhaps he was a mockery, perhaps he was an abomination. His evolutionary biological drives were dependent on this process; there was no coupling for his species, and before he had digested Larry he had never felt a keen desire for it, nor had he ever felt a revulsion for his own natural ways and impulses. His species' way was to kill, to murder. To abhorrently take a life for one's own benefit. Before he had digested Larry he had within his line's ancestral memory no understanding of morality. To kill meant nothing to him because meaning had yet to exist within his comprehension as an abstract. Now imbued with moral agency, he felt he was forced to question everything, and did so in ways stranger than he felt he could ever have understood. He reasoned with examples and metaphor and simile and thought experiments. He considered that a cancer cell kills not from hatred, but wondered whether it could continue to do so with such cold indifference were it to know what it did, and while he considered this he marvelled and simultaneously felt horror at reason, and what it was to think.

Come Saturday night, Larry had not slept since birth. He had an overwhelming urge to spawn; to catch the train into the centre of population where he could guarantee the most branching; to release his hold on this strange bipedal form; to explode outwards in a sea of spores that would lead to more lifetrees, more sap cocoons, more mockeries, endless lines, branches that would branch, and branch again; to fulfil his biological drives more successfully than in any other environment in which his line had ever been. The only price to do so would be the human race, and the only cost genocide.

Humans were a devastating creature to be, and to be an evolutionarily driven parasite one day and a grown man the next was jarring. He had learned more from being Larry in two days than his line had learned in a millennium. He had a responsibility to his species, but he hadn't understood responsibility until he had been human; so, in a sense, did he not too have a responsibility to humanity? There was no knowing if he was the last of his species—his lifetree may well have been the only one seeded out of the great blackness that was space. Did this matter? Did he have a responsibility to his species beyond evolutionary drives? And what of mankind? And what if he did spawn?

Would it be a monstrous cruelty to not only destroy mankind, but in doing so condemn all who branched from him? They would all now carry Larry's knowledge and convictions. His convictions. Their convictions. They would all know and feel what he had done, and know and feel that it was wrong. They would know what it was to kill and to have killed and to want to kill again. Was it worse to fail your obligation to a species and not reproduce, or worse to reproduce and in so doing condemn all who followed to carry the experience of slaughter and genocide?

Larry had liked being himself, and now he, despite being a mockery, despite being just the latest link in the longest of chains, found that he liked being Larry. He liked to laugh, and to think, and to talk. He now enjoyed food—and not just for its nutritional necessity—and he now felt affection beyond that which was biologically driven. He had learned more from this form than the combined knowledge of every link in his ancestral line before him. He had learned of love, thought, self-awareness, and kinship.

He had also learned about combustible materials.

No other creature predating him in his line had ever had a sense of duty, but he felt keenly that if he were to abandon duty, those who followed would be forever tainted with self-loathing by his failure to act. Larry had only worn the facade of humanity for two days, but now saw himself as more human than anything else, and felt himself a threat to mankind and all that he loved. He was the monster that the man whom he had digested feared as a child; he was the plague that nightmares warn of; his species was the harbinger of death to all who thought and loved. He was a mockery, a perversion, and an abomination.

His line could not be allowed to branch.

The gasoline Larry doused himself in would be enough to kill any spores that escaped his burning corpse. He doused himself for the friends he had never met but remembered fondly, for the girl who loved what he wished that he was, for the parents who were proud of achievements he remembered but had no part in, and even for the football team he supported but had never seen the game they play.

Knowing that with him his line would end, but that mankind would live on, Larry Carol lit the flame, and sat below the tree that had birthed him.

THE CRABS OF MORAHT ISLAND

For the longest period of time the island of Moraht existed only in legend. Its location, like many places during the Age of Exploration, was always tentative and uncertain, relegated to the edge of maps. Much like the exact location for the Garden of Eden, the sunken city of Atlantis, and the home of the Amazons, the island was always speculatively placed just beyond any searcher's reasonable grasp. However, just as the Great Southern Land Mass, the Americas, and Greenland would attest, not all lands that were rumoured and speculated about were content to remain mere myth. Between 1534 and 1742 Moraht Island was "discovered" multiple times by multiple nations, was given several names and had been dedicated to several monarchs; all the while it continued to shift on maps to various (though slowly narrowing) geographical locations. Due to fibbery, fanciful storytelling, and outright incompetence it was not until 1867 that Moraht Island was finally reliably placed, and its natives brought into the modern world of global commerce.

Despite the mythical nature of the island having been largely reduced, fables and tall tales would always persist when sailors were involved, and Moraht Island was spoken of readily in any dockside tavern. While some yarns these sailors spun were contradictory, it was generally agreed upon that the people of Moraht Island were exclusively youthful and beautiful, that on the island it never rained, and that the fruit that grew there was plentiful and especially sweet. While all these claims were heard by most with at least some level of scepticism, one fact about Moraht

Island that was undeniable was that the crabs that grew in the small tropical location were the largest, fleshiest, and tastiest in the region, if not the world.

When rumour had first spread of these crabs, profiteering quickly followed, and traders found that they were of a size that could easily feed a whole family. These large dark-blue freshwater crabs proved sturdy enough to weather sea voyages, and without difficulty could be kept alive in tanks to be sold fresh in fishing ports globally. More importantly, they were in high demand and, much to the delight of traders, the locals of the island were all too happy to exchange them for decorative gems and costume jewellery. With no real concept of their worth, and with the crabs being extremely plentiful on the island, they quickly became Moraht's main (and only) export.

Despite the purchase of these crabs costing traders little more than faux jewellery, the expense of transporting them from the island to civilised ports was something that many sellers hoped to cut down on. The common solution sought out by these entrepreneurs was to attempt to breed the species locally; however, doing so proved impossible, with even the first generation of offspring growing to an unimpressive size no larger than any other found throughout the tropics.

Kanan Trundle was one such trader and hopeful breeder. While most would-be farmers of the Moraht crab quickly gave up on the notion of breeding them, and instead turned to securing larger storage vats for more profitable journeys, Kanan held to the belief that local breeding could be achieved. By the time that Kanan began to make his arrangements he was—so far as he was aware—the last profiteer and entrepreneur still taking steps to solve the breeding issue.

The others, Kanan thought, were merely content to quit after their attempts had failed. He, however, was not so inclined to accept defeat. He had done the calculations and he was certain that the profits to be gained from a local supply of these crabs would far outweigh any expense. He had also become convinced that, as offspring of the exported crabs were unremarkable, then it was something about the environment in which they grew or their diet—not their species—that caused them to grow to such a size. Realising this, Kanan prided himself on being the first Moraht crab trader that was logical and adventurous enough to have chartered a ship to Moraht Island, not to trade with the locals, but instead to discover the native secrets behind the crab's growth, and to learn exactly how it could be replicated back home.

If any sailor aboard the *Minerva* were asked how they felt their voyage to Moraht Island had gone, they would likely describe it as "pleasant" and "uneventful". They would no doubt talk of calm seas and relaxing weather. They, of course, were viewing the journey through the eyes of experienced seamen who had seen poor weather and truly knew what on the ocean could be qualified as "eventful". In light of this, they would no doubt disagree with Kanan's somewhat dramatic account of "mountain-high waves" and "winds that could strip the paint off a sign".

Kanan—despite having lived his whole life in a shipping town and having made a living from acquiring, fishing and breeding seafood—had never before this voyage actually been out to sea. It was not long into the journey that he had begun to suffer sickness, and started to wish that he had maintained his lifelong record of staying on dry land. He had even solemnly sworn to the captain on arrival at the island that he would never again set foot on board a ship and had (for the briefest moment) considered the virtues of island living when the captain had snarkily asked if he would be, in that case, cancelling his return voyage. Kanan had fortunately composed himself enough to think better of becoming a permanent resident, and the return of the *Minerva* was organised. Even so, despite his regained composure, Kanan still had to restrain himself from kissing the sand upon disembarking the small rowboat that had taken him ashore.

It rained heavily that night, and the small wooden hut that the natives had provided him with was far from waterproof. On arrival he had been greeted curiously, welcomed, and led inland to a small settlement. Through trading some of the locals had developed a basic understanding of English, which was fortunate, as Kanan had no grasp of their language whatsoever. He had brought with him some trinkets to give in thanks for their hospitality, and was amused to learn that, of what he had brought, they held gold in less worth than coloured glass. It further amused him that a people whose exports had made so many others so very wealthy kept themselves to such basic living. The settlement mainly consisted of small huts that were sporadically placed around a large freshwater lake, which Kanan could well imagine would be crystal clear were it not for the heavy downpour. Though the dryness of the island in myth had clearly been somewhat overstated, the friendliness, youth and beauty of the natives had not been. Due to their kindness, Kanan held his venture in high prospects. They were, to Kanan's excitement, not only happy to host him, but even appeared eager to share their knowledge—though they did not seem to fully understand the concept of farming.

As Kanan watched the rain fall on the lake he considered his position and took stock of his adventure. He had travelled further than he, his parents, or his grandparents had ever gone, and was now in regions that were to him just as uncharted as the island on which he now stood had once been to the civilised world. It was unknown exactly how long he would reside here. He would leave when the *Minerva* returned, though that could be (depending on their trading, the sea, and the winds) anywhere between two and six months. It was a wild adventure and a wild gamble but, if the natives really were as friendly as they seemed, and as willing to share information as they claimed, then it would mean a pleasant stay, and great wealth for him upon returning home. Kanan began to again do the maths in his head of how much he could stand to earn from this venture based on the current sale price of the crabs and by the breeding speed of their diminutive offspring. Suddenly Kanan was startled out of his contemplation by a native who, he noticed, was standing in the doorless entryway to his cabin. The man smiled at him in a friendly manner, and informed him that food would soon be available.

"Available food" to Kanan was somewhat of an understatement, and he made a note to himself that he would have to teach the native the term *feast*, as a feast was exactly what was served. The spread was set out on large green leaves placed on the shore of the freshwater lake. Beside them was a large fire, which burned unhampered by the rain. The meal consisted of many varieties of fruits (some of which were entirely new to Kanan), as well as fish, eels, turtles, and to Kanan's delight giant crabs, all of which were being cooked in the fire.

There was some form of short ceremony that one local did his best to translate. From what Kanan could understand from the native's broken English, the feast stood both as a "farewell and good luck" to three members of the tribe who, having reached their twenty-fifth years, would tonight be making a pilgrimage to an area of the island with some spiritual significance. The feast was also—rather flatteringly and embarrassingly—in honour of Kanan, by a way of welcoming him as a guest.

Kanan partook heartily of all that was provided, though he especially paid attention to the crab. It tasted even better, and seemed even fleshier, when farmed so fresh and so locally, and he had several helpings, followed by several more.

Some kind of native wine was served, and he drank and they drank and there were drums and dancing and food and wine.

At one point the food ran low and, with a spear, a native expertly brought up another crab from the lake, despite the lake's depths being invisible due to the whitening from the rain. The crab was added to the fire, and more wine was served, and they continued to eat, and they continued to dance, and they continued to drink.

As the evening rolled on, Kanan consumed more wine and ate more crab, and the night blurred into a sea of stars and raindrops lit by moon and flame, and eventually he awoke to the morning sunshine and his regrettable headache.

The rain had stopped and the lake outside was crystal clear and as blue as the sky that shone down upon it. The fresh air was especially inviting, so Kanan decided to walk along the banks of the lake, where children swam, women weaved, and men fished.

Kanan stooped and collected a pebble, which he skipped along the lake and watched its ripples grow, distort the water, then clear as the pebble slowly sank its way to the bottom, settling itself amongst the crabs, and the bones.

Bones that were so many and so vast that they stretched the entirety of the freshwater lake, becoming almost lost amongst each other—without scrutiny they would have appeared as nothing—but bones they were.

Bones that shifted as the crabs moved amongst them.

Giant crabs that grew here larger than anywhere else in the world, due either to their environment, or their diet.

The friendly natives fished and weaved and swam. They were all young and beautiful, and to them such large crabs were not unusual, and to them the bones were no spectacle.

The crabs congregated and shifted and moved over one another, and fought for the supremacy of the meal.

Some fought over skeletons where mere morsels of flesh were left to cling.

But most clambered and tore at the remains of three men, who, having reached their twenty-fifth years, had been celebrated and farewelled, and had undertaken their spiritual pilgrimage.

STREAM OF CONCIOUSNESS

t's all digital; that's all it ever was. The hardware was fleshy and the programming language naturally formed but, when it all comes down to it, a brain is just a computer, and a mind is just a mess of ones and zeroes.

There were several companies leading the way to fully maximise man's potential in the fields of cloning, neural enhancements, and synthetic replication. Astral Industries, one such company, was narrowing their focus on the mental, hoping to expand thought well beyond the confines of one's own skull. Brains, and even whole people, were possible (though not inexpensive) to replicate—a simple body scan and a sample of DNA and you could create a synthetic copy of a person in minutes. This copy was, however, merely of their physical form—an empty shell, physically identical to that from which it was scanned, but blank and entirely devoid of thought, knowledge, personality, and sentience. Any attempts to replicate human consciousness or to imprint artificial intelligence onto a synthetic human brain had thus far proven unsuccessful. In order to circumvent this issue many laboratories were experimenting with the use of natural consciousnesses with synthetic clones, by either uploading or streaming the natural consciousness into the replicas. In *Astral Industries* these experiments were being headed by one Dr Charles Laythan, assisted by Dr Julian Epi.

"Are you sure it can handle it?" Dr Epi asked, looking at the disembodied clone of Dr Laythan's brain.

The pinky-grey organ floated in a vat, and was connected to a life support system, a small light, and a linking cable that ran to Dr Laythan. Their experiment was still in its infancy, and before the company would be willing to invest the finances for a full-body clone they would need to establish the feasibility of *Conscious Streaming* through interfacing with a standalone brain. If they were successful, the synthetic brain and Dr Laythan's natural organic one would (for the duration of the experiment) share Dr Laythan's consciousness. To prove that his consciousness had been effectively interfaced between the two brains, Dr Laythan's goal in this first experiment was to simply use the secondary brain to blink the small light. That was, *if* they were successful. The experiment, to be successful, was dependent on a lot of strange technology that she and Dr Laythan had had to make work together, and between the exposed brain and strange wires, it all looked a little too much like the set of a B-grade horror movie for her scientific tastes. For a moment Dr Epi stared at the brain and considered what Descartes or Harman may think of all this.

"It should handle it. *Synthka* are using similar neural copies, and word has it they've already achieved an upload; we're weeks behind," grumbled Dr Laythan.

Dr Epi shuddered. She considered the theorised one-way nature of *Mind Uploads* that *Synthka Laboratories* were reportedly experimenting with as too invasive to ever achieve mass public appeal. It involved the wholesale permanent transfer of the mind into a synthetic body, and the disposal of the original. *Astral Industries'* technique, however, Dr Epi believed *did* have potential for a public market. The idea was simple. By using your own brain as a host, neural amplifiers would allow you to broadcast your own consciousness into a second compatible brain (which in turn would broadcast back), allowing you to literally be in two places at once. The idea of *Conscious Streaming* was often outlined to investors as being akin to remote control, but it was more than that. Much as the two hemispheres of a brain already work together to form one consciousness, while the two brains were linked, thoughts would be created in both and relayed to one another. You were, *during the period of interface*, just as much the synthetic copy as you were your natural self. The benefits of *Conscious Streaming*—if perfected—would be great. The need to travel would become non-existent as your mind could go wherever a compatible neural clone of yours was printed and, when such neural copies were placed into sturdier bodies, dangerous jobs could be carried out with comparative safety.

"Well," Dr Epi said as she ran her hand along the thick cable that connected Dr Laythan's thought-amplifying helmet directly into the synthetic brain, "do you think this cable will be able to handle such an intense stream of data?"

"One way to find out," said Dr Laythan. A vacant expression fell across his face, and then a smile, as a small light on the other side of the room began blinking green.

Case Notes. 23-5-2083

Dr Charles Laythan.

The sensation of being beyond the bounds of human form is a strange one, and one that I'm not sure I'll ever forget. I did not, as I had expected to, feel as though I was in two places at once, but instead as though I was both in one place, and no place. This should perhaps have been expected. My brain copy was, after all, without any sensory inputs. My consciousness' second location was entirely, therefore, without any ability to ground itself spatially. Intellectually I could see it from my natural form's location with my own eyes, and knew myself to be also where I glanced, but there was no sense of my being there, beyond the sense of being an indistinct "elsewhere".

With no sense of smell, scent, or hearing that second non-place felt emotionally cold and alien. Despite this, while I had no sense of control or understanding over how I blinked the green light, its being only connected to my second brain shows that blink it I undeniably did.

Further experiments will require the brain to be equipped with extra sensors to test out the sensation of physically inhabiting two locations at once. Today's success shows promise; thus I

request the funds and means to achieve full-body
cloning in order to continue.

It had been two weeks since their first experiment, and now Dr Laythan stood staring at a naked copy of himself, then at his actual lab-coated original self, and then the naked self again. Bridging the two was a cable that ran from Dr Laythan's thought-amplifying helmet directly into the skull of his copy.

"What are you feeling?" Dr Epi asked, staring at the strange spectacle.

"I feel as though I'm in both places, and my vision—" Dr Laythan began.

"—is swapping between me and my clone," his clone finished.

Dr Epi noted with interest that it had been the clone Laythan that had spoken second, despite it having referred to the original Laythan as the clone while doing so.

"Can you tell which is which?" she asked.

"I can, from the sense of where I am—" Dr Laythan began.

"—and what I'm looking at," the clone finished.

"I am the clone looking at my natural body," said the clone.

"And I am the original form looking at my clone," said Dr Laythan.

"Do you feel you are inhabiting one locale more than the other? Can you control which is receiving your attention at any given time?" asked Dr Epi.

A long pause followed.

"With effort," the synthetic finally said.

"It is like staring at an optical illusion: if you concentrate hard enough you can choose to see either the duck, or the rabbit," Dr Laythan's natural form elaborated.

Dr Epi took some notes.

"Can you see through the eyes of, talk with, or feel that you're in the presence of both simultaneously?" she asked.

Both the clone and the original furrowed their brows in concentration; then, suddenly, the clone fell to the ground and Dr Laythan slumped against the wall, panting.

Case Notes. 5-6-2083, Dr Charles Laythan.

To call today a total failure would be as dishonest as to call it a complete success. I have been in two bodies at once. The sense of smell, hearing, and spatial awareness was felt in both bodies simultaneously. The ability to move, speak, or see was something I could only handle through one body at a time. Whether this is due to a need to practise or because of a weakness in the clone is, as of yet, uncertain.

And now the bad news. In the process of the experiment the clone was worn out. Its synaptic nerves are totally fried. We have run a scan on my brain (the original), and fortunately no similar damage has been done. This would indicate a weakness or fault in the clone vessel, not the process at large.

Another attempt will be made following refinements in the cloning process.

Dr Epi stood behind a one-way mirror and observed two of her colleague, divided by a small partition wall, performing their tasks. The real Dr Laythan sat in his lab coat on the floor, legs crossed as though he were a Buddhist monk, wearing an expression of intense concentration. The second Dr Laythan—the clone—only visually different by the red overalls it wore, performed simple tasks. Both sides of the room were entirely soundproofed from each other, and only the real Dr Laythan, not his synthetic clone, could hear Dr Epi. It was then up to the original form to send the thoughts and instructions to the clone form beyond the barrier. They were no longer utilising a heavy cable in order to maintain the *Conscious Streaming*, but instead a wireless interface that drew upon considerable power.

"Now pick up the ball, and stand on one leg," Dr Epi instructed.

Dr Laythan paused, nodded, and his clone seconds later followed the instruction.

"Now hop on one leg," said Dr Epi.

"You're enjoying this, aren't you?" asked Dr Laythan while his clone followed the instruction.

"Where are you right now?" she queried.

"I am here, and I am there," said Dr Laythan.

A screen turned on in the room of the synthetic clone, and began to slowly cycle through colours.

"Please list the colours you are seeing."

"Red... green... blue..." began the clone.

"Give the list from your organic form," she corrected.

A pause, and then Dr Laythan began from his original self:

"Pink... orange... blue... purple."

They were all correct, and Dr Epi excitedly noted down the accuracy.

"Now, answer me simultaneously in both bodies, if you can: who wrote The Odyssey?"

"Ho-mer," both the natural and synthetic Dr Laythan said in a strange drawn-out unison.

"What is two plus three?"

"Fi-ve," they both spoke again.

"For whom do we work?"

"Astral..." began both, but the clone collapsed and Dr Laythan finished, "Industries," weak and alone. He paused to catch his breath.

"Time?" he asked.

"Three hours, seven seconds—same as last time," said Dr Epi.

Case Notes. 29-6-2083, Dr Charles Laythan.

Our latest experiment has shown that the mind can handle functioning while sharing two separate locations. It has also proven that wirelessly streaming the consciousness from the host brain to the clone brain and back is feasible, though it does require considerably more energy than the wired form. While connected to the secondary brain it does not feel as though one is primary, but instead as though my consciousness is evenly shared, evenly produced, and inhabits both neural networks—natural and synthetic—equally. I suppose, in a very real sense, it does and it is only my familiarity with my natural form that allows me to keep the two distinct.

Basic sharing of tasks and multitasking done by both my original form and my synthetic copy were attempted. It is achievable, but requires heavy concentration. Imagine it as an extreme version of patting yourself on the head while rubbing your stomach and counting backwards. With practice I expect it to become easier; it is, it seems, all about mental discipline.

The clone forms are still failing to last much longer than three hours. Perhaps the synthetic material used should be more aimed at strength, rather than at accurately replicating the organic form. Dr Epi is looking into the possibility, but until then we prepare to test the potential distance of wireless conscious-streams, and will, as of Monday, be finally utilising Site 2.

"You realise that, in order for this to become commercially viable, we will probably have to discover an alternative energy source?" mused Dr Epi.

Their previous experiment had involved merely streaming consciousness across a small room. The giant generator she now began to prime would create many times more power than they had used for that experiment. Across the city, where the latest Laythan replica was located, sat a second, equally powerful, generator. The two systems would allow Dr Laythan and his clone to wirelessly connect and remain connected for the three-hour span of the clone's projected functionality. In doing so they would use more power than the entire city within which they were located would normally use over the course of two years.

"Ready?" asked Dr Epi.

"Ready," confirmed Dr Laythan.

"Bringing it all online," said Dr Epi.

A loud buzz and hum followed, and gradually Dr Laythan regained the strange, yet now familiar, sensation of being in two places at once, and relaxed down into his comfortable seated position.

"Describe Site 2," requested Dr Epi, notepad in hand.

"The walls are a light, almost toothpaste green; it has the same generator set-up we have here, but is painted red; there is a large screen mounted on the wall."

"Good," said Dr Epi.

Dr Laythan had never been to, or seen, Site 2, and his description matched it perfectly.

"The screen will now begin displaying images. I need you to tell me what they are," said Dr Epi, and keyed a sequence into her own machine to begin the process.

"A boat... a cat... a bridge..."

"Good."

"A plane... a mountain... a horse."

"Good again. Now, have your synthetic self walk counter-clockwise around the room that it is in."

On Dr Epi's video feed she watched the clone do just that.

"And now you—if you can—with your original form walk around this room clockwise."

Dr Laythan struggled to his feet, stumbled somewhat, and then began walking. For a moment the synthetic copy changed direction on the video feed, then both went anti-clockwise, and then, with effort, Dr Laythan achieved having both of himselves moving in opposite directions, on opposite sides of the city.

"Good," said Dr Epi. "Now—"

There was a sudden smell of copper and burning wire—and then blackness, and Dr Laythan found that he was lying on his back in the dark, staring up at the ceiling. The sensation of being in two places at once had been severed.

"Julian... what happened?" asked Dr Laythan disoriented. For a moment no reply came whatsoever, and then a robotic voice spoke.

"Back up generators online," it reported, and the light on the ceiling flickered on to reveal a green-walled room and red-painted generator. Dr Epi was not present—but then again, of course she wasn't. This was, after all, Site 2.

This was bad news. The connection to his original self had been entirely lost, and now his full consciousness had seemingly somehow been transferred into his synthetic copy. A copy that was—judging by all previous experiments—not long for this world. And then there was what he had smelt, and the reason behind the disconnection, which troubled him further. There had been burning, but nothing here at Site 2 was burnt, and so the burning odour must have been from Site 1. The large generator dedicated to the experiment at Site 2 was still running, but the site's lights (connected to the city's power grid) had gone down. Had the whole city lost power, and had this somehow affected the experiment, or had the experiment gone down, and somehow affected the whole city's power? If there had been a problem with Site 1's generator, it is possible that it could have tried to draw power from (and overloaded) the city's power grid, which would explain the loss of lighting here. It would also mean serious problems for Site 1, and for a brief moment Dr Laythan allowed himself to worry for the health of both Dr Epi and his currently uninhabited natural body.

A thought suddenly occurred to him. Had he lost consciousness when the connection was severed, and if so, had he lost precious time?

"Computer, when did we lose access to Site One?" he asked.

"Connection to Site One was lost one hour and forty minutes ago," came the response.

Dr Laythan swore, tried contacting Site 1 to no avail, and then rushed outside to flag down a taxi.

"Astral Industries, Site One, fast," he ordered with urgency.

"I'll get you there, but it won't be fast; every traffic light in the city is down, yah know?" came the response.

"Make it fast, and I'll double the fare," he pleaded, and the taxi sped up, yet even so over twenty minutes of precious time was used navigating the dark streets of the city before finally arriving at Astral Industries Site 1. Instructing the driver to bill the company, Dr Laythan ran from the vehicle up the driveway of the building and in through the foyer, acutely aware as he did so that his synthetic body was already on borrowed time.

"It should be as simple as doing a cabled reconnection with my vacant natural self," he outlined to himself as he forced the powerless doors to the laboratory open.

Theoretically it shouldn't be possible to do what he planned, but until recently he wouldn't have believed his current predicament possible either, and so held on to hope. The doors struggled against his effort, then finally gave, and smoke along with a sense of helplessness washed over him.

The generator hadn't just burned out. It had blown—and in a big way. Shrapnel, fire damage, and still burning flames littered the laboratory, and what appeared to have once been Dr Epi lay sprawled and scorched in the corner.

"Who's there?" a weak voice called out, and Dr Laythan felt cold sweat run down his back. The voice belonged to a second bloodied form, pinned facedown by a heavy sheet of metal.

"It's me, it's Dr Laythan," he responded to the voice.

"What?... but..." the voice trailed off.

Dr Laythan approached the confused form, removed the heavy covering, and turned the figure over to confirm the unsettling theory that had been building within him since entering the laboratory. The second form—bloodied and broken—was that of the original, organic, Dr Laythan.

"How. Are—are you ful—" the original began.

"I am fully sentient... I thought... I thought we were transferred to this clone body... but it would seem I was duplicated... we split," the clone theorised.

The original was struggling to move, and his synthetic copy bent down to try and help him up. When he winced in pain it became apparent that there would be no moving the original Dr Laythan, and so his copy instead stayed sitting beside him.

"That... that shouldn't have been possible..." the original Dr Laythan coughed painfully. "If the lab equipment wasn't so destroyed we could have tried re-syncing... tried becoming one again..."

"There... isn't much to return to," the copy weakly assessed.

The original let out a laugh that quickly turned into a painful cough.

"That bad, eh? We... always were too honest, weren't we... How much time do you have left?"

"I... likely have less than a minute," said the clone.

"Me too, I'm afraid," agreed the original.

As they sat together, the fire continued to burn, and seconds passed.

One coughed and went silent, and the other began to slump, and within the destroyed laboratory of *Astral Industries* two identical doctors—once one—shared together in two distinct and individual deaths.

THE PAVED GRAVES OF VERAS

Veras is a small flat town with pleasant people, several bakeries, and an impressive Gothic church. Surrounding the town are small green hills that are connected to one another through natural caves and tunnels and are sporadically decorated with trees. The fresh drinking water of Veras is provided by a clean river that neatly winds its way through town and has never been prone to flood. In 1813, a notable lord commented when passing through Veras that "the town of Veras has some of the best bakeries in all of England" or at least such is claimed by the bakers of Veras. Veras has many minor pleasantries that make it, like many such similar towns, a nice place to live, and a good place to visit.

Unlike many such similar towns, however, Veras boasts one peculiarity that sets it apart from all other towns in the country, and perhaps the world.

The cemetery of Veras is entirely paved over.

It was this peculiarity that sparked the interest of Tobias Shnykt, PhD, in the small town. Veras was intended to be nothing more than one of many stops on his journey—travelling by carriage, train, and on foot—on his way from London to Edinburgh. The professor arrived late in the afternoon and with no further travel services until morning intended to simply pass the night in Veras, before heading off to the next town at sunrise. Upon his arrival the sun had not yet set, and the town appeared picturesque enough. Never one to waste an opportunity, Tobias—often finding that small towns had interesting untapped histories—set off to explore the village.

Ever a student of architecture and history (both modern and classical), Tobias Shnykt decided to first explore the town's wall. As he walked it he pondered whether it was Roman in design or medieval in origin. The stone structure was only one pedestrian wide, but circled the entire town, breaking only in two places to allow for the river to run through. It was from this raised viewpoint on the wall that Tobias first saw the town's cathedral, which stood tall in the centre of the village and seemed well worthy of investigation. Thus, having completed his circuit of the town, Tobias decided to make his way directly towards it.

The church impressively towered over all other structures in the town. It was built of dull-yellow bricks, but had been blackened heavily on its western side where some catastrophe had apparently caused fire and extensive damage. As well as the scorch marks that appeared to have spread from floor to ceiling of the church's westward fronting, one of its three western buttresses—likely during the same incident—had broken away. It appeared this damage had happened some time ago, as no signs of fire could be seen in the church's surrounds, and the broken buttress itself had been cleared from the area, evidenced only by the broken stone to which it once connected and the lack of symmetry its absence created.

The cathedral—a plaque out the front informed Tobias—had been built in 1489. It was capable of seating eight hundred people, and was constructed from heavy Bath stone. However, as imposing as the structure was, it managed to be completely overshadowed by its surrounding cemetery.

Red Brick Cemetery—imaginatively named for its red bricks—sits in the centre of the town, and surrounds the aforementioned Gothic cathedral. As Tobias explored the paved cemetery he became increasingly perplexed by the discovery that, despite the age of the town, all grave markers found within the cemetery seemed to be dated no earlier than 1542. This fact grew all the more strange when paired with Tobias's knowledge that the area in which Veras stood had been hit by a particularly devastating plague in 1541, and so should have had no shortage of corpses to bury from that year.

It was, he thought, a possibility that the deaths from the plague had been so many that the cemetery he stood in now had been established afterwards, due to the first cemetery becoming over-capacity. This held, except for the fact that, generally speaking, a town's first cemetery would be located within the town limits, and subsequent ones moved further away due to the town's growth. Tobias had never known a new cemetery to be built in the town centre, let alone surrounding a cathedral that predated it by half a century. And never before had he seen a cemetery that was entirely—from path to grave plot—paved over.

In stark contrast to the grey and white stone of the church (and indeed the grave markers), Veras's Red Brick

Cemetery was made of the same clay-red bricks that ran in its streets and footpaths. Evidently, the graveyard was still in use contemporary with Tobias's visit, as when he looked out amongst the graves he observed several markers from the current year, and noted that within the grounds there were unpaved unused patches of dirt as well as tarp-covered bricks piled near what must surely have been the undertaker's hut. His curiosity piqued, Tobias decided to put off the next leg of his journey by a day and return to the cemetery early the following morning. By doing so, he reasoned, he may be able to witness the town's strange funerary rites and learn of the mystery behind the paved graves of Veras.

On arrival the next morning Tobias found himself morbidly grateful that a funeral was set to take place. A fresh grave had already been dug by the undertaker—despite Tobias having arrived just after sunrise—and, as he watched from a respectable distance, mourners slowly began to show, and the ceremony commenced. Tears were shed and words were spoken; it wasn't until the funeral was coming to a close that it began to differ from others that Tobias had been unlucky enough to have had to witness in the past. The coffin was lowered and dirt pushed on top. An elderly couple (presumably close to the deceased) then approached the grave and each placed a red brick touching where the grave marker met the exposed earth. The ceremony now seemingly having drawn to a close, the party departed, and the undertaker began to properly smooth the dirt and plant the remaining bricks. By the time he had finished, the new grave was seamlessly connected to the rest of the paved cemetery.

The undertaker was an unkempt-looking man with a dirt-sodden face. Tobias waited at his observational distance for the party to properly quit the gravesite, then approached the man and enquired about the strange practice.

"I just do what I'm done told to, nothing more, nothing less," the man responded slowly.

Tobias left his enquiry of the man at that, but was told by two schoolboys who had—while cutting through the cemetery on their way to class—overheard his questioning, that the pavements were "to stop the Landys". Tobias was familiar with many terms in many various professions, but had never once before heard the term *Landys*. Before he could ask further questions of the boys, the ringing of a school bell was heard, and the young students fled towards the schoolhouse.

There would be no train to leave the town until late evening, so Tobias decided to allow the full day for further investigations. If the gravekeeper was not privy to the reasons behind the paving over of graves, then, Tobias figured, surely the church's minister must be. Following this line of thought, Tobias made his way into the cathedral itself with the intention of questioning him. There was no indication in the minister's spirits that he had only just finished presiding over a funeral, and he greeted Tobias with warmth and kindness. This warmth however, quickly dimmed and seemed less genuine when the visitor enquired of him as to the reasoning behind the paved cemetery.

"It is customary to do so," the minister responded shortly and in a manner that indicated no follow-up questions were wanted, or would be answered.

Tobias saw that questions about the cemetery were a dead end, and instead turned the conversation to the question of what exactly it is that a Landys was. At this, any facade of friendliness that had remained fell away completely.

"This is a house of God," the minister replied in a harsh whisper, before asking Tobias to leave.

Similarly Tobias found unwillingness to help his search at both the town centre and the library. Staff and officials at both locations gave no indication of the reasons behind the red bricks, refused to comment on "myths" when asked about the Landys, and only drew up short of denying entirely that a fire had happened at the churchyard at all by stating that "no records of any such fire" exists. No explanation given by Tobias that he was a researcher with the University of Edinburgh, nor his insistence that his questions were purely academic, sufficed in preventing rejection. It was, at this point, fairly evident that if Tobias were to find information on the reasons behind the red bricks or the meaning of the Landys, he would have to look to less conventional methods. If all respectable members of the community were tight lipped about the situation, then he must seek out less respectable witnesses. It was this avenue of thinking that saw Tobias Shnykt, PhD, heading to the town tavern before it had even turned midday.

Despite his early arrival at the establishment, a handful of gentlemen were already settled in and, judging by their conversations and volume, had already been patronising the venue for several hours. Tobias approached the bar, ordered a pint, and asked the bartender if there was anyone in the pub that was willing to talk history, and was friendly to strangers. At this, Tobias was promptly pointed towards one Bill Kan, and was assured that the man was willing to talk friendly on any subject you could wish of him, and that the larger difficulty was not in making him talk, but instead in making him stop.

The man indicated—Bill Kan—was a portly gentleman with a dark-grey moustache and a pipe. Tobias approached him where he sat alone at one of the tavern's small circular tables. The glass he was drinking from was joined by three other empty mugs and, when Tobias asked if he could join the man, Mr Kan found he had to burp before he could give a response.

"Sure enough, 'course you can!" replied Bill, pulling his glasses towards him in order to clear a space for Tobias's mug.

"I hear you are the one to talk to about local lore, and the history of Veras?" Tobias enquired.

"Sure enough," he agreed again. "Closest thing to a professor here in Veras, I am!" he bellowed, and a few of the patrons laughed in response.

"Good, good; well, I'm doing a study," responded Tobias, and the man drew an almost comically serious expression, and leaned closer over the table while nodding.

"A study on Veras?" he asked

"Yes, primarily on the red bricks, and their origin," answered Tobias.

"Ah," he said shortly, and drank the rest of his beer in a single action. "Folks don't like it when you talk about that, you know?" he carefully noted.

Tobias placed his beer next to Bill's empty one, and Bill eagerly picked it up and took a sip.

"Yes, I asked the minister about the Landys, and he asked me to leave the church."

Bill laughed into the mug, and placed it down with a thud.

"Sure enough, he would have! Sure enough at that!" he exclaimed.

"So will you tell me?" Tobias pressed, and the man smiled.

"You buy me and you the next round, and I'll tell you, sure enough I will." And he did, sure enough.

Despite the bartender's dig at Bill's tendency to overtalk, from the moment Tobias went over and enquired of the story behind the red bricks, and the meaning behind the strange word *Landys*, all in the bar, including the bartender himself, went quiet and began to listen. Bill had finished the beer given to him by Tobias as quickly as he had downed the one preceding it, and, with the next two drinks being brought over, he wiped the white suds off his grey moustache, and began to relate his tale.

"Just as we do now," he started, his voice becoming deep and mysterious, "Veras has never had more than one undertaker at one time, and those we've had since have never worked so hard as the one we had in 1541."

"The plague," another man commented knowingly, and the teller gravely nodded, and repeated the comment before continuing on.

"That bum—Tod Harris—you would've saw him today, he wouldn't had lasted back then, sure enough he wouldn't have. He's five descended from the one we had back then though—Jack Harris. It's always been the same family tending graves here in Veras.

"The plague was bad in 1541. Dozens were dying every day. No man can dig a dozen graves a day in frozen dirt, and so Harris—Jack that is—well, he took to collecting them—the dead—every morning. He took them in his wagon, and he said he had found a place with softer dirt outside of town he could bury them in. People weren't too fussed with watching burials then anyway, not when corpses could carry the plague and spread it, so no-one asked Harris too many questions about where he took them. They didn't know he was dumping them in the pit outside of town usually reserved for trash—it isn't there any more, so don't go looking for it, but back then it was a stinking hole of rotten, putrid flesh and bone.

"As I said, they didn't know he was doing this at the time, but they eventually learned, and they were not happy at that! Many folk say even now it was wrong of Harris to do this—disrespectful of him to dump their loved ones in with the trash. But bodies kept mounting, and no-one was offering to help dig (and he asked), so Harris, he kept dumping them, until one morning he took his wagon to the pit …"

"—and it was empty," another patron cut in breathlessly while the others nodded solemnly.

No other talk was going on in the bar, and all had gathered to listen to what must be a favourite sordid tale of the town. Even the bartender, as he continuously wiped down the same long-dry glass, watched and listened to the tale.

"That's right," Bill agreed, beginning again. "Empty, or at least empty of flesh and bone, sure enough it was, but the trash was still left there, you see? Left completely untouched, just the bodies gone."

"What about the markings?" chimed in a patron.

"Yes, the markings!" another agreed.

Bill took the moment of intrusion to take a large drag from his pipe and, while he did so, Tobias turned to the first of the two to have interrupted, and asked what he had meant by "the markings".

The man, a skinny gentleman with yellow-stained teeth, responded eagerly to his moment in the spotlight: "In the side of the ditch there were two large gouges, cut, like something heavy had climbed in, you know?"

He had accompanied the word *cut* with a large emphatic hand gesture.

"Aye," Bill agreed, taking the cue. "There were big gouges, and deep footprints leading back into one of the hill caves, sure enough," he added, nodding sombrely.

Tobias thought on this for a moment. There were always rumours of bears and mountain cats in these areas, but he had never seen any of them himself, though he was not sure he doubted their existence.

"You mean to say," he said, "that an animal took the bodies?"

Such enquiry was met with laughter.

"You're not understanding how biggen it was," Bill responded, "We're talking footprints you and your fattest girl could lay down in! Not something a wild animal could make, but a beast! But we're not there yet!"

This time it was Tobias who took a large drink from his pint, and leaned in closer to the table, eager to hear what more Bill had to say.

He began again: "So he—Harris, the undertaker—he saw what he saw, and he told what he'd seen to those folk back at town. Everyone was furious to learn where he'd been dumping the bodies, but the elders—when they heard of the tracks and of the bodies being gone—they were especially mad. Mad and scared.

"They grew real scared, and started to speak of creatures in the caves. Well, they told him that such creatures were drawn by death, and that Harris, in doing what he did, had invoked one. It sounds silly, but they were deadly serious and, I'll tell you, most the folk here are still the same way when asked about it. Sure enough, they are."

"So I've seen," said Tobias, and Bill nodded a grunt in response.

"But as I said, they were real mad, and the townsfolk were furious about the dumping and the bodies going missing. Well, Harris—he was having none of their criticism, and he said he had dumped the bodies where he did 'cause he had to, and that he would keep doing as he was until others were willing to help. They grumbled plenty, but what could they say? One man can't dig twelve graves a day in frozen dirt. So from then he was joined by others in the community of good health to dig graves in the frozen earth, rather than Harris digging or dumping alone. They dug the graves in the afternoon when the ground was most thawed, and then buried all the new dead first thing in the morning, so the town would be satisfied that the dead weren't being disrespected, and the elders wouldn't worry about what's in the caves."

"The screams," added one patron quietly.

"The screams?" asked Tobias

"No—well, yes, but not until the next night," the bartender grumbled gruffly in correction.

"Sure enough," agreed Bill. "As our host says, this next morning Harris, with their help, collected the corpses and buried them by the church where we had buried the dead since the town was founded—even before the new church replaced the wooden one in 1489. Well, that was all well and good, but he was still curious about the ones he had put in the ditch the day before. He hadn't brought those ones back to town—you see—when he saw that the ones before them had gone missing, he had dumped them anyway. What else was he supposed to do? Bring a wagon of plague corpses *back* into town? So curious he was, that before the new dead from that night were even buried—before anyone had even awoken to help him—Harris had snuck back out to the ditch to see if the bodies from the night before last were still there or not."

"The Landys," breathed two of the men at once.

"The Landys?" repeated Tobias curiously.

"Yup, plain as day, the Landys was still in the ditch, feasting on the rotten plague flesh from the day prior. By Harris's account he heard its slurps and bone crunches even from his distance!"

There was a respectful pause, which, after a moment, Tobias broke the silence, asking, "But what exactly *is* a Landys?"

All five men turned to look at him with shock. The description of a Landys offered to Tobias came in fast succession, with each person present giving different elements of the creature's parts that made its whole, as though they were all too excited to describe the creature in its entirety:

"They're long! Longer than they are tall!"

"Pitch black, all over, with white eyes!"

"Short back legs, long front! They move like wolves, but run like horses!"

"Claws, sharp claws."

"Pointed snout that curves to the floor and tapers narrow!"

Bill was nodding along with each of the descriptors, and once they were expelled added: "Landys are attracted to death and disease; they are drawn to it, like ants are to sugar, and in turn they spread it. Any malady that a corpse has suffered, when devoured by a Landys, will become a part of it—and this Landys had tasted plague, and so plague was now part of this Landys."

"*Now* the screams," reaffirmed one of the listeners.

"Yes, now the screams," agreed Bill.

"You see, the Landys is drawn to death; it has a great sense of smell, and that mass grave had drawn it out from whatever depths it lived in. It was real fond of the feast we'd been putting out for it those last few nights, and when it came the next day only to find the pit corpseless—well, it wasn't happy, sure enough it wasn't.

"And that's where the screams come in, you see? They say the Landy doesn't only take on the malady of those it consumes, but also takes on their voices too, and when it saw that there was no food left for it, it screamed with the voices of all those it had eaten. So loud was its scream that they could hear it all the way back in the village—hear it and recognise that it was all those that were dead they could hear yelling, and know that it couldn't be them, all the same.

"Some blame Harris for what happened next. They say that it tracked him—his smell, the smell of death he carries. Some say it tracked that back to the village. I say this is hogwash; the Landys can't just smell death, but dying too, and once it was out from those caves—up in the fresh air— sure enough, it could have smelt the dying in the village without help from Harris, I say."

The four patrons were silent, and for a spell it seemed they would say no more. In an effort to lift the spirits and grease the wheels Tobias bought another round, this time for all present, including the bartender himself. After placing the beer in front of Bill, he softly commented to himself "well, sure enough", before beginning his tale once more.

"There was a commotion that night, but no-one left their homes to see what was making it. After all, half the village was quarantined anyway, and the other half knew all too well what they might find if they looked, and so didn't. But in the morning they had no choice but to look. The sun was coming up and the bodies of those who hadn't made it that night were starting to stink, and so they had no choice but to look. They had to look, and what they saw was that they would have to handle the corpses themselves, because Harris hadn't been by to collect them, and certainly wouldn't, you see?"

At first Tobias had assumed this was a rhetorical ques- tion, but then it became apparent that the conversation would progress no further until he answered it.

"Harris was dead?" he offered.

"Sure enough," agreed Bill. "The Landys had come to Veras, you see, because there wasn't nothing else to eat back in the pit, and it had gotten real hungry. It became plain to all that this were the case when some did venture out, only to find the cemetery defiled, houses with their doors knocked in, and the groundskeeper's house destroyed. Just lucky his wife lived in a different house, or he'd have been the last Harris, I guess.

"Well, anyway, you see, the Landys has that long snout, so it can stick its nose right through doors, windows—walls, even. It laps up the festering dead right from their death-beds. And with its claws it had violently exhumed and defiled half the graves. Harris hadn't been dead—not before the Landys had gotten to him—and he hadn't been dying neither, but he was a good groundskeeper, and we reckon he tried to stop this sacrilege of the church grounds, and that's why it went to the effort to get him."

There was a sombre pause, and all had a drink. Tobias felt he now understood the point of the tale, and how it explained the graves, and so attempted to venture his guess.

"So that is why the cemetery is paved?" he asked, "To stop this creature from violating the sanctity of the dead?"

Bill laughed.

"For the dead? No, not hardly! Sure, people cared about the dumping in the pit, but that was when they had time to be concerned about such things! 'The sanctity of the dead'—*as you say it*—is a privilege that the living only care about when they themselves are safe, and this weren't that!" he cried.

Tobias was confused, and maybe even a little offended by the claim. He felt that a good burial was the right of any good citizen, and that this right was owed regardless of the prosperity of the times. He did, however, not wish for his offence to end his investigation and so, swallowing his pride, asked, "The pavements are not for the dead?"

"Surely not! The pavement is for the living! You remember I said the creature carries plague? Well, once it has found a food source, it will keep returning. Twice as many people died that night the Landys came, and it would come again precisely because they did! The Landys don't like to eat the living. Oh, it will kill if it has to, as poor Harris would attest, but it likes its meals to be nice and rancid, and because its coming brought plague, and because plague brings death, well, so too did its coming assure its return!"

Tobias nodded slowly as he began to fully comprehend the issue. "So how does a town, once plagued by a Landys, possibly rid itself of one?" he asked.

"Do you know how we keep pests—rats and the like— from eating our food scraps?"

"You poison the scraps," replied the bartender.

"Aye, sure enough," agreed Bill, adding, "Our host could tell you all about rat problems, I'll bet," at which a few of the patrons laughed, and the bartender muttered a few obscenities.

"So, the corpses were buried in the cemetery as you'd expect—but all in a mass grave—and with them all the oil from our town's lamps, and all the gunpowder from all our powder kegs. Then, a sacrifice was had to be made. You see, all those already sick with plague were the ones who went out that evening to deal with the Landys, while those still healthy stayed in and hid. The unsick couldn't risk coming in contact, because if they did, they too would catch whatever the Landys was carrying, and so it was the sick that went out, and the healthy who stayed in and hid. The healthy claim this was done by choice and volunteering, all noble like, if you know what I mean, but I sometimes wonder. The Landys prowled through the town, and the townsfolk had to watch all quietly as it headed for the church. Twenty-seven had died that night prior, and they—the sick—had to watch as it approached the mass grave, and watch as the creature sucked down and crunched each of the dead. They dared not move until it got dead-centre, you see, centre of the grave, where the biggest load of explosives was piled."

Bill went silent. Tobias was unsatisfied.

"And the beast was killed?" he prompted.

This time, Bill did not laugh.

"You can't kill a Landys, but you sure as hell can hurt one! That blast knocked the beasty backwards into the church—knocked down one of its pillars while it did! That you *can* still see if you look today, you know? And it—the Landys—tore around the cemetery all burning and screaming in the voices of all it had eaten. Real hell fury, you know? Then it ran into the hills while still alight, and that night the hills around Veras burned.

"We reckon it ran back into its hole, you see, because the whole hillside was alight with the fire that night. All who had taken part in the killing of the Landys died. Most died from the plague, some died from other sicknesses that the creature must have been carrying, but those that died that evening—they were the last victims. That was late December, and it was the last day of the plague of 1541, and the Landys hasn't been seen since, though sometimes we hear its screams, and know it's still out there.

"It's still out there, and so the pavements have been done ever since, as a precaution. It knows where we are, and it knows where we keep our dead, so we make sure they're hard to get to, and we know it remembers that we are not an easy mark."

With that, Bill's story had come to an end. The group fell silent and did not seem quite so jovial as they had been when Tobias had first entered the pub. Tobias thanked Bill for his tale and bought him, the bartender, and the four others one final round before leaving.

The story was, of course, Tobias reflected, totally fanciful, and nothing more than a window into the collective mythic culture of those who live in Veras.

Even so, when walking through the paved Red Brick Cemetery on his way to the small train station that after-noon, Tobias couldn't help imagining a Landys pawing at the graves, or how it might have looked while rearing back, aflame, into the soot-damaged side of the cathedral, causing one of its great buttresses to break and fall.

And when finally that evening Tobias Shnykt, PhD, caught the last train out of town, he was certain that amongst the wail of its whistle, and the roar of its engines, he could just make out the sound of screams faintly echoing their way from the surrounding hills and their natural caves.

BOEHM LIGHTS

Duncan awoke to the wet tongue of a stray dog. It was light out. He wondered how many neighbours had already seen him and had walked past *tsk*ing. Duncan must have gotten drunk again, though he couldn't remember the preceding night, and swore (not for the first time) that he would never drink again. He sat up and patted the dog absent-mindedly, his head spinning.

Boehm was the kind of small South Aussie outback town where everyone knew everyone, population 260-ish. At one point, long ago, it had had its boom with the gold rush; now it was just small businesses supported by small locals. Some old ladies walked by and warmly wished Duncan good morning, and some young boys prepared to play a game of marks-up around him. For a moment Duncan wondered if it was rude of them to play with him there, or if it was rude of him to have fallen to sleep in the town's park where they intended to have their game.

"Why don't you move on home so the boys can play?" Mr Baker, the town's pastor, called out from the footpath.

"I was thinking I'd head to church," Duncan threatened lightheartedly.

The pastor walked over and offered Duncan a hand up.

"You, in church? That'd be the day!" he laughed.

"Really, Pastor, I've turned my life around. I've even stopped drinking!" Duncan replied earnestly.

"Easy enough to stop, but will you be staying stopped once the pubs reopen for the day?" he asked.

"Now, how would our good barkeep feed his kids if I did a thing like that?!" said Duncan aghast.

The pastor laughed and congratulated Duncan on his charitable works, before farewelling him, and turning to go. As he turned Duncan caught his arm.

"One more thing, Pastor," he said. "Did something... happen last night?"

"Happen?" said the pastor. "Like what?"

Duncan paused.

"I'm not sure," he said. "Something bad," he added.

The pastor stopped and thought, ruffling his brows as he did so, straining to remember the night prior.

"Yes," he finally said uncertainly. "I think something did," he agreed.

Farmer Lawry's cows were wrong. There were 134 head of cattle on his farm. Not all cattle look alike—it takes a farmer to know that, and these cows *looked* like his cattle all right, but they acted... wrong.

It wasn't how they walked, or how they interacted with one another, or him, and it wasn't even how they mooed, but there was something wrong about them that Farmer Lawry couldn't quite put his finger on.

"Coffee, dear?" his wife offered, and Farmer Lawry took the cup with thanks and had a sip.

"Something seems different," she commented, looking out across the field.

"Cows are wrong," agreed the farmer.

"Sleep well?" she asked.

"Nup," he said.

"No, nor here," she confessed.

"Hmmm..." pondered Mr Lawry.

"Weird day," assessed Mrs Lawry.

"Weird day," Mr Lawry agreed.

Superintendent David Tarrence played with the small die-cast police car on his desk, and wondered for the thousandth time why he bothered with a uniform. There were only two cops in town, him and his sergeant and everyone in town knew who they were. The trousers of their uniform were too warm, and the powder-blue shirts too clearly displayed his sweat stains, and he knew he would be more comfortable in a pair of shorts.

It was going to be a slow day. It usually was, but today the phone hadn't even rung once. He shouldn't be expecting trouble; the only troublemaker in town was Duncan, and he'd still been asleep on the lawn as David had passed him on the way to the station. Knowing Duncan, he would be far too hungover to cause any trouble for a good six hours now anyway, and yet...

And yet?

There was something that made David feel uneasy. He wasn't sure if it was that the phones hadn't rung, or because he had slept so poorly, or maybe it was those dreams that he had had...

Sergeant Pat Jones entered into the small doorway and knocked on the doorless frame.

"Superintendent?" he said.

"What is it, Pat?" asked David, noting the worried expression his sergeant wore.

"Julie's just been by. Mayor says the phones are dead," he said. "Looks like they're down for the whole town," he added.

Superintendent David Tarrence swore.

Being the mayor of a small town was hard. Everyone knew you, where you lived, and what you looked like. The townsfolk that had voted for you would always tell you they had, and expect stuff, and those who hadn't would always tell you they hadn't, and wouldn't be shy about saying why. Any small issue going on in the town was "exactly the kind of reason you didn't get my vote" from someone, and today, the phone lines were down.

"Did you know the phones are dead? Last mayor never let the phones go dead!" was the third time he had heard of the issue this morning.

"I voted for you, Mayor, and I'd really appreciate it if the phones were fixed by six tonight—my mum's expecting a call," was the fifth.

"Probably didn't pay the phone bills; I've always said you looked like an embezzler," was the ninth.

The lines were dead.

He was well aware of that now, and really, what did these people expect him to do about it? He wasn't a telecommunications expert, and there were none in town. It wasn't like he could phone the phone company! As soon as his secretary had arrived at the office he had sent her to the police, and then on to see what was going on in Mosel, the next town over. But Mosel was four hours away. Four hours there, and four hours back, and somewhere in between she would have to find out what the problem was. Chances were, she would have to sleep in Mosel, and wouldn't be back until morning.

There was a knock at the door, and the mayor called for them to come in.

"Mayor, did you know the phone lines are dead?" the visitor reported.

It was going to be a long day. He wasn't even sure who these farmers and store clerks were so eager to call anyway. The police hadn't even realised the phones were down until he had sent Julie to tell them.

"Thank you, I know," the mayor grumbled tiredly.

"I'm sure you'll get it fixed soon," she said. "That's why I voted for you," she added.

It wouldn't be so hard to deal with such things if he hadn't suffered such a poor sleep, and from so many strange dreams, but as it stood, he had, and now the phone lines were down, and he could feel a headache coming on.

Until nightfall, Sunday in Boehm progressed in a manner not dissimilar to any Sunday in Boehm before, marked apart only by the unplaced quiet nervousness felt by many of the townsfolk. Pastor Baker had preached apocalyptic doom, inspired by recent night terrors, to an unusually full church. Duncan had knocked back his usual nightly intake of beer as early as 3 pm, hoping to forget things that he couldn't quite remember, and Superintendent Tarrence had had to send Sergeant Jones past old man Stevens's house after hearing reports of him battening down the windows as though he were expecting a storm. And on the long stretch of road that ran between Boehm and Mosel, Julie Herrington was becoming increasingly panicked.

She had been driving for hours. Her morning had started late, having overslept following particularly restless dreams. While trying to call in to inform the mayor that she would be late for work, Julie was the first to learn that the phone lines were down. Once in the office, and having informed the mayor, Julie had been sent to tell the police, and then to drive to the next town over. It had been roughly 1 pm when she had finally hit the road to Mosel—a four-hour drive away from Boehm, and now she had been driving for four and a half hours straight, with no sign of the town in sight. Boehm had long since disappeared behind her, and she was now flanked on either side by endless desert, with nothing but road stretching before and behind.

"There should have been a service station two hours ago," she said aloud to herself.

"I should be in Mosel by now," she added.

"I should have never left Boehm," she whined.

The sun was beginning to set too soon, and the stars above were starting to blink into existence, and Julie began to grapple with the unpleasant realisation that she would soon be driving alone at night through the endless outback.

"You took a wrong turn," she said to herself, knowing that this could not be the case.

There was only one road to Mosel, with no turn-offs, and she had taken it.

Julie began to nudge the accelerator closer to the floor, edging the car over the speed limit. She now wanted to be in Mosel more than she wanted to avoid a fine, and even welcomed the prospect of a speeding ticket, seeing as it would mean a police officer would have to be present to issue it. Above her, one star glowed, and glowed brighter than the rest. It became as a midnight sun, and it tracked and followed. Julie sped up and slowed down and the star copied her actions, and grew until there was no road, no desert, only the light.

Back in Boehm the sun had started to go down, and some commented on how it shouldn't be setting for another few hours. The cows weren't happy about it either, and Farmer Lawry was equally concerned. Night fell and he stood staring up at stars that were not his, and understood why the animals had been off. His wife joined him, and asked if he would be coming to bed, and what was the matter.

"The stars..." he said, and his wife looked up.

"Where is the Southern Cross, and the Big Dipper, and the moon for that matter?" she asked, confused.

"Where are we?" said Farmer Lawry.

Monday morning came to Boehm, if that's what it was, and that's where they were, and a town meeting was quickly called, with most of the locals making their attendance.

"Why are the phones still down?!" a lady shouted.

"That's not why we're here," said the mayor, though he conceded it may well be related. His secretary, Ms Julie Herrington, had awoken in her own bed, and with her car in the garage, and nothing but a near-empty fuel tank to attest to her long journey.

"Things have been weird this last day... or two," began the mayor, "and this meeting aims to figure out why, and what can be done," he outlined.

"Weird how?" asked a lady.

"We're being watched!" yelled old man Stevens, causing Julie to shudder.

"The stars are wrong," added Farmer Lawry firmly.

The mayor pleaded for people to be orderly and to speak only after having raised their hands, "classroom rules", he had stressed to light nervous laughter.

"Now," he said, "Pastor Baker has reported a lot of you have been having dreams. Don't worry; he didn't say who, and you don't have to name yourselves, but there have been a lot of you, and I've been having them too... and I don't remember Saturday."

Silence fell across the room as many present turned pale or ashen in realisation of their shared memory lapse.

"Does anyone remember Saturday? Raise your hands if you do."

No hands were raised.

"There is also the matter of the stars; as Lawry just called out, they're not what they're supposed to be... they are not stars you should see in the Southern Hemisphere... or anywhere in the world, for that matter."

Someone swore, and another yelled that they had to get out of town. The mayor took a deep breath.

"There is also something stopping us from leaving—some kind of light," he admitted.

Panicked arguments broke out across the hall, and refused to be silenced. The mayor, once they had run their course, opened up the floor for more formal discussions. One demanded the military or federal government be called, forgetting that the phone lines were down; another suggested group prayer, but even the pastor (while offering further church sessions) thought further steps must be taken. Eventually it was decided a car would be sent, driven by Superintendent Tarrence (and paying no attention to speed laws) along with two passengers with the hope of getting to Mosel before sundown—before the stars came out. It was agreed upon, and they left immediately, with

Sergeant Jones riding shotgun, and Farmer Lawry in the back.

With the car dispatched, Boehm's day progressed in a way that—to any outside observer—might seem perfectly normal. However, if you knew the town you likely would have found it strange that so many were at church on a workday, or that no children were at school—or even playing outside, or that old man Stevens was not in his garden, but instead was sobbing quietly in his kitchen. Nervousness had overtaken the town, and the vividness of their nightmarish dreams of hellfire stalked even their waking memories. The pubs were full of men trying to drown them out, while Duncan, the bar fly, had not turned up, and was instead drinking at home, where he hadn't stopped since Sunday.

As night fell, nervousness became hysteria under the veil of strange stars and absent moon. Everyone stood in the streets looking upwards, hoping to spy familiar lights in a vast unrecognised sea, and all bore witness to the one light that appeared, grew, hovered over, and then entered into the house of old man Stevens.

On the road, the three sent out encountered a similar light. Night had fallen early, and they, despite having not once slowed below 120 kilometres per hour, never reached Mosel.

Farmer Lawry had been brought along for his familiarity with the stars—a familiarity that proved just as pointless as the bullets they fired into the strange light that descended upon them. Each officer emptied their full clips, and Lawry unloaded his shotgun, and all of them awoke the next morning at home in bed.

No town meeting was initially called on Tuesday. Hysteria was too widespread to get much value out of everyone being present. In the mayor's office stood Julie, the mayor, Superintendent Tarrence, Sergeant Jones, Farmer Lawry, and old man Stevens.

"You're all here because you have had an encounter with the entity," began the mayor.

"Entity?" gasped Jones.

"Whatever it is has purposefully stopped us from leaving town; that would suggest intelligence," agreed Superintendent Tarrence.

"And the phone lines," pointed out Julie,

"Yes," agreed Tarrence, "it also doesn't seem to want us communicating."

"It means to isolate us," reflected the mayor.

"But... why did it go into Mr Stevens's house?" asked Julie,

Old man Stevens looked embarrassed.

"I—uh... I tried to hang myself," he admitted. "The dreams, you know—I couldn't handle them, so I hanged myself and woke up in bed."

"But that's good!" said Julie.

"Julie," began the mayor shocked.

"Not the hanging, but that whatever it is wants us alive," she clarified. "It wouldn't let Mr Stevens die," she added.

"It won't let us leave, but it also doesn't want us dead…" mused the mayor.

"So… what do we do?" asked Sergeant Jones.

"We use that to our advantage," said Superintendent Tarrence.

At this, a town meeting was called, and a heavily armed Superintendent Tarrence, Sergeant Jones, and recently (and unofficially) deputised Julie and Farmer Lawry made sure all—even the heavily intoxicated Mr Duncan—attended. Once all were present, the doors were sealed and the townsfolk were informed of the planned hunger strike to force the entity's hand.

"They won't let us leave, and they don't want us harmed, our well-being is our only bargaining power," the mayor explained to boos and hisses.

One man yelled out that the mayor would never be re-elected, and another grumbled that they wished they'd had a bigger breakfast. As night fell, one young man attempted to rush Sergeant Jones, and was promptly sat back down for his actions with a hard kick to the gut. Come morning, none had energy enough to mount a coup, but still complained plenty. By the beginning of the second night even the complaining had ended.

And then came the brightness, and the voice.

"You must seek nourishment," it stated matter-of-factly, the room pulsating brightly with each word.

"We refuse," responded the mayor.

"You will cease to be," it warned.

"That is our choice, just as living, or leaving this place, should be," replied the mayor.

The light dimmed and flickered, then flared back up.

"There is nowhere to leave to," it stated.

"We wish to go to Mosel," said the mayor.

"There is no Mosel," came the response.

People had forgotten their hunger, and whispered murmurs to one another in fear at what they had heard, and what they were hearing.

"How did you change the stars?!" blurted out Farmer Lawry.

"The stars have not changed," said the voice.

"Are we... are we in Boehm?" asked the mayor.

"A perfect replica," said the voice.

"Return us to the *real* Boehm," the mayor demanded.

"Impossible," returned the voice.

"Then we will not eat," threatened the mayor.

"You must be preserved, and so you must eat," said the voice.

"They mean to make pets out of us," Julie whispered, horrified.

"We are not creatures for your amusement, and we demand you return us to Boehm, to Earth!" cried the mayor.

"There is no Boehm; there is no Earth," said the voice.

Silence fell across the hall, broken suddenly by old man Stevens.

"Oh god... the dreams," he whispered. "Tell me they were *just* dreams... The fire, and the blood... Say that they are not memories," he pleaded.

The room filled with fruit, bread and jugs of water.

"You must eat," said the voice, "your species must be preserved," it added.

THE WELL OF MANOR HILL

The house on Manor Hill stood as lonely as its owner, and looked down towards the drought-stricken town below. From his vantage point George could see the townsfolk going on with their lives. Most minded their own business. They walked in the streets and stopped to speak to one another. They entered and exited stores and they went in and out of their homes. George never went to town unless it was absolutely necessary but his wife had gone there far too often, and for that George despised them and her.

It hadn't rained for months. The grass was dying, the trees were wilted, and the town was thirsty. Many had owned the property on Manor Hill since antiquity, but for the last century it had belonged to the Fagle family— currently George Fagle and his wife. A bloodline that, much like the town that the old house overlooked, and the well that George stood next to, had seemingly run dry.

Not all within the town below were content to go about their lives minding their own business, however. Instead, some seemed intent on bothering George. Some, George saw—*police officers by the looks of them*—had left the cobble-stone streets of the flat town, and were making their way up past the dying grass and the wilted trees, and over the narrow winding dirt road of Manor Hill, towards George and his home.

He cast a sideways glance towards the old well uneasily, and awaited the officers' arrival.

"I suppose you heard Tom Mickley's gone missing?" the constable asked.

"Ran off with my wife, I'm sure they say," grumbled George.

"No, *they* say your wife and he were to live in town, but he and she are *not* in town, and *he's* gone missing," said the constable.

It sounded like an accusation.

"I hadn't heard that they weren't there; I don't frequent town," said George plainly.

"But they're not here?" asked the constable.

For a second George impulsively glanced at the well, but caught himself, and instead stepped onto the wooden plank that was covering it, making as though he had simply wished for a better view of the town.

The town looked dry.

Had the constable noticed his glance?

"You must think me very amicable, and Tom Mickley and my wife very brazen, for you to suggest that they're here," observed George.

"So not here?" said the constable.

"No," said George.

"So elsewhere?" he ventured.

"Yes, elsewhere," agreed George.

"*If* elsewhere, then where might she and he have gone?" pressed the constable.

"She, like Tom, has gone missing," said George matter-of-factly.

The constable joined him on the wooden covering of the well with two *thump thumps* of his feet, and looked down at the town.

"Dry," he assessed.

"Yes," agreed George.

"You covered the well," said the constable, tapping his foot.

"It gave no water, and was a hazard. Don't want people falling in—after all, I'd be liable... and with it having no water... it is very deep, after all," said George.

"Covered for safety," summed up the constable.

"For safety," agreed George.

"Prudent," assessed the constable.

The constable stepped off the well, and made back towards the path.

"Let us know if you hear from Tom and your wife," he called out.

"Surely," agreed George.

It wasn't long before George heard from Tom and his wife.

It had just turned midnight, and George was awoken by the mournful moans and painful screams of his wife, and the man with whom she had left. It sounded as they had when they did, but as George slowly became fully conscious, he realised it was not all as it seemed.

It was just the wind.

Just the wind—but somehow more than just the wind. The trees quaked and the windows rattled, and the gusts wailed, and screamed, and moaned, and while George knew it was *just the wind* he felt sure that it was somehow more than that, and while he knew that the gale that raged did so all around him, he was certain that it came from the old well.

Entombing himself in the pillows and blankets of the bed that he had once shared with his wife, George tried to hide from the sound—the screams, and the moans, and the wails. George tried to convince himself that no matter how accusative the storm sounded, and regardless of how human and with how much pain the winds cried, that it was indeed all just a storm, but try as he might his convictions wavered and failed, and soon he was driven out from the warmth of his bed towards the front of the house, and to the window. George looked out and saw the old dry well—exposed and bare. Gone now was the wooden covering, *blown down to town, no doubt*, and from deep within its depths it screamed and moaned and wailed accusations. Accusations that *must* be silenced—lest the whole town hear them.

George opened the door, and struggled through the cries and the wails and the screams towards the well, and upon reaching it, looked down to see... darkness.

The winds were not from the well—of course they weren't.

They were from all around—*it was just a storm.*

Peering down into the well, all that George could see in its depths was blackness—the night was too dark, and the well was too deep, and there was nothing in the well capable of making such sounds. Uncovered as it now was, nothing could be seen, and all was still hidden, and so it was back to a warm bed and reassured sleep.

He closed his eyes and tried to forget the screams, and the old well.

It was just the wind; it was just a storm.

No-one would go looking into the well in the middle of the night, and if they did it would be too dark anyway, and wherever its covering had gone it could be resealed in the morning.

2 am came, and once more George was awoken suddenly—this time not by wind, but by loud *knocking*.

Knocking on the door, the window, the roof.

Knocking on the very ground outside.

But who would knock at this hour?

The police?

Had they heard the wind's screams? Had they looked into the well?

From the bedroom to the window again George rushed, and looked out, and for a moment was confused by a sight long since gone from the dry town. There was no knocking, but instead the heavy pelting of raindrops all over the house, the hill, and the town below.

It *rained*, it *stormed*, and still the trees quaked and the windows rattled, but no longer could the screams, moans, and wails be heard over the endless cleansing rapping of the heavy downpour. It was a rain so heavy that it may as well have been biblical. A rain to wash away the dust and the sin, and to quench the thirst of the land. George once more returned to his bed reassured.

It was now early morning—just passed 6 am, and George was awoken once again to loud *knocking*—knocking joined by knocking—both the rain, and something else.

There was a *knocking* at the front door, distinct, and different from the pelting rain.

George felt cold and fearful.

Leaving the safety of his bed one final time George went to the door, turned the handle, and felt it blown in by the scream, felt himself soaked by the wet, and startled by the man.

In the darkness it was momentarily and impossibly Tom Mickley—but then he spoke—and it was the constable, accompanied by two more officers and handcuffs for George.

"Your wife and Tom returned to town," said the constable.

George found it impossible to stifle a gasp.

"They—they couldn't have," George stuttered, his eyes wide with fear, and then wider with realisation.

Beyond the door and over the constable's shoulder George could see the front yard—puddled and flooded, and George could see the old well: full, and overflowing.

It was then that George knew and understood.

Knew that the old well—dry no more—had filled, and floated away those once deposited within.

Had washed them down past the dying grass and the wilted trees, and down the narrow winding dirt road of Manor Hill, and back into the small town below.

NO TIME FOR PAST DISCRETIONS

y the end of year 2137, the great plague—begun five years earlier—had already claimed the lives of eighty percent of Earth's 11.3 billion inhabitants. Despite the best efforts of scientists, and constant hopeful reports from the media, no cure had yet been developed. There had been attempts to slow the spread. Homes were quarantined, then streets, towns, cities, states, and countries. Eventually all borders were closed, and all movement outside of your immediate vicinity restricted. Ultimately efforts to slow the spread proved futile, and the mounting sick and dead resulted in the total collapse of global agriculture, trade, and economy. However, where medical science had failed, technocrats had thrived, and they, along with the combined help of Earth's governments and the wealthy, had constructed the *Ark*.

The imposing superstructure that was the *Ark* would, to any earthbound observer, appear as a second, smaller moon. Up close it looked nothing more than a giant ball of glinting silver. This sphere, much as its biblical namesake would suggest, was built to ride out the proverbial flood that had soaked the world. Its literal use, however, was to allow for those housed within to remain apart from the world, taking refuge inside a time-sealed temporal-distortion bubble for the period of one thousand Earth years.

To those housed within the *Ark* a mere month would pass, but to those outside the influence of the structure's fourth-dimensional warp-drives, *true time* would pass unhindered. Despite the vastness of the structure's 100-million-person capacity, well over two billion of Earth's inhabitants would—upon its temporal departure—be left behind. This was, of course, regrettable. It was, however, also unavoidable, and furthermore it was entirely necessary. It would have been both financially and materially impossible to build a structure large enough to hold all Earth's inhabitants. Furthermore, were all Earth's inhabitants brought along for the thousand-year journey, it would defeat the *Ark*'s purpose. After all, in order for those within the *Ark* to return to an Earth that had defeated the plague, rebuilt the economy, and hosted a society that had regained its mantle of civility, there must, by necessity, be those left behind to rebuild. For generations those below on Earth's surface would grow, struggle, develop, and die, while above them, unchanging, hung the *Ark*.

The *Ark* had it all. It was in a very real sense a fully functioning city, created with the intention of a mere month's usage. Its populace was split roughly seventy to thirty, with the smaller proportion making up the politically, socially, and economically important members of society that had either paid (or been gifted) their place on board, and the larger seventy percent making up the staff. The jobs that occupied the time of this larger percentage of people ran from chefs, pool boys and cleaners (all placed for the enjoyment of the guests), to engineers, doctors, and scientists (whose responsibilities were more focused on maintaining the vessel).

The staff were not in for a cushy journey. They, unlike the guests, had not paid to be on board the *Ark*. Theirs was not a pleasure cruise, and they were expected to work. They would receive payment for their month of work, but it was generally expected by those who employed them that they should consider the destination (rather than any monetary gain) as their true payment. As for what they were paid, they would be receiving no more than a single month of standard income, which, before their departure, had been invested for them in Terpons's Banks, and would be collectable upon their arrival. They were told that this investment will have grown significantly by the time they returned; however, it was also boldly underlined in their contracts that there were no guarantees on this matter. Much like the truth of a utopian future that had conquered disease, poverty, and suffering, what their investment in the year 3137 would amount to, or even whether Terpons's Banks (and currency at all for that matter) would still exist, was the subject of mere speculation. The risks did not end there. Joining would also mean leaving behind all of what, and who, any potential staff member knew. However, as much of what they knew was already in desolation and most of who they knew were already dead, there were few who, despite the uncertainties, didn't apply for a position all the same.

One such application was lodged by Wendy.

Wendy was a nurse, and a damn good one. As she looked around at the other medical staff in the conference room of their onboard hospital she saw many others that she would similarly classify.

They couldn't have left many good doctors behind, she noted to herself as she recognised much of what made up the remaining pandemic response team around her.

The man who stepped up to the podium was Dr Wilton Thwip. He would be—he informed them—the head doctor on board the *Ark*. Yesterday he had been the head doctor in the largest remaining public hospital. He cleared his throat, and looked out across the medical staff.

"We've just got to keep these bastards alive for a month; after that, on the other end, there's either a cure, or there isn't, and either way it's on them," he rather bluntly stated.

His short speech having concluded, there was no applause, but some murmurs of quiet agreement ran their course. By rights, their expertise would not be needed beyond any regular pre-plague requirements (broken bones, heart attacks, the occasional ingrown toenail), and Wendy longed for the days in which that would be the case. In reality, however, their encountering the same plague that had so heavily afflicted Earth was almost a certainty.

It wasn't that there had been no precautions. Careful measures had been taken to ensure that all those who boarded the *Ark* were healthy and free of disease. Despite this, even at the best of times, detecting the plague was diffi-cult. In some it ran asymptomatically. Even then, if they had been detected, it was practically accepted that there would be those who worked to cheat the system. They were, after all, working with the wealthiest and most powerful of humanity, none of whom wished to be left behind. These were people who were used to always getting their way, and it wasn't long before rumours began to spread of bribes having been issued to hide positive test results and to green-light those who should have been immediately quarantined or denied entrance to the *Ark* entirely.

Due to this, it surprised no-one when, mere days into the journey, positive tests began to be widely returned, and the plague began to spread rapidly throughout the *Ark*.

Morbidly this new outbreak gave Wendy a strange sense of homesickness. The sixteen-hour days and nine-day weeks she found herself working were practically identical to what she had been doing while earthbound for over four years. It was, perhaps, only distinguishable from her life pre-transfer because she now shared a large dormitory with nineteen other nurses (rather than being one of the last living residents in an apartment building), and because her clientele (rather than consisting mostly of the poor working class) was now (excluding her fellow staff members) entirely made up of the elite, and the entitled. She did not enjoy serving them, but looked forward to the possible prospect of practising medicine in the more normal circumstances of the proposed future.

"I'm not worried—I've got strong blood. Strong blood," John Terpons boasted to Wendy as she took his temperature in the overly large room in which he was staying.

"I won't be testing your blood," Wendy responded tiredly, placing a swab in the man's mouth.

It was the beginning of week two of their four-week journey, and the plague had already been detected in more than a quarter of those on board. It was spreading most rapidly through the staff due to the shared spaces in which they lived, and this appeared to be of little concern to the higher-ups, so long as it was contained from the majority of the guests. So far Wendy had been one of the lucky ones, and had thus far managed to avoid infection, though she felt as though it was only a matter of time. Over a dozen of the staff on board the *Ark* had not been so lucky, and had already died—or were in the process of dying. They had lived, while on Earth, in extreme poverty and were now dying while treating people with single items of clothing worth more than their combined debts. And yet, on their deathbeds, many expressed hope that if only they could hold out a little longer—*just one month, or a thousand years*—then they would be cured.

"Nergh therth sterh," the man said as his tongue fought with the swab.

Wendy sighed and removed it.

"Didn't quite catch that, sir," she replied to his mumblings.

"Not the tests; blow the tests, I said!" he said.

"Oh yes? Blow the tests," replied Wendy, inserting the swab into a small vial and watching for colour changes. John Terpons had already tested positive and quietly it was assumed that he was patient zero on the *Ark*. If the vial turned blue it would mean that Wendy would know to start treating for organ failure.

"My blood, my boy, my *lineage*!" John said proudly.

The vial turned a dull blue, and Wendy readied a needle. John frowned.

"Bad, eh?" he asked.

"This shot will give you a good fighting chance, but there are no guarantees," she admitted.

"Ah," he said, pausing. "Highly contagious, you know. You probably have it too, chances are!... How long do we have?" he added.

"Results vary. You might beat it," she offered as weak assurance.

Wendy had seen too many tens of thousands die in too short a period to have managed to maintain her bedside manner. Despite this, he took it well, and perked back up.

"Sure we will. Good blood, my lineage. Boy's left in charge of the company, you know! When I come back there will be one thousand years of growth there! A thousand years! Good businessman, he is... I only have to survive a few weeks—that's to be expected—then the cure, right?" he said looking up at her.

"That's what they say," agreed Wendy, jabbing him in the arm with the needle.

He jumped and tensed slightly at the ice-cold feeling, and then with effort relaxed himself once more.

"He's handsome, too, my boy. I'll probably own a continent when we're out!" he added.

Wendy excused herself from the room. She had many more patients to attend to today and over the next two weeks. They were all sharing a similar mindset. They seemed not only completely convinced that the benefits of a healed world would await them, but also carried a strange certainty that there would still be a place for them within it. They spoke of family members left behind as though they would see them again, and expected to just step back into their lucrative careers, strut the stage of the silver screen once more as world-class performers, or be given back the helm of the companies and countries they had led as though they had simply taken a four-week sabbatical.

Wendy was less convinced, and felt they were deluded to believe that the world would wait for them to the degree they expected—or at all. When they returned, she thought, there was a risk that those they had left behind would regard them as ancient history, if anyone would be there to still regard them whatsoever. Even so, despite simultaneously finding their confidence and arrogance absurd, and even vulgar, Wendy still found it difficult to not share in it. After all, the success of the venture, and the success of the guests, was directly tied to her own and the staff's. While she held it unlikely John Terpons's company would be waiting to take him back with open arms, she also shared in the pipedream that her wage—invested in his bank—would grow, and allow her easy living on her return, and she hoped that the utopia they imagined would materialise just as they predicted.

Was it so wrong and greedy to hope and even expect these things? Wendy wasn't sure, and yet found herself daydreaming of them regardless of their likelihood.

Whatever the case, whatever it was the future would hold for them, it *surely* couldn't be worse than the past that they had left behind.

Could it?

After Wendy's allotted five-minute break, her next patient was Janice Thorton—"*The* Janice Thorton", as one of her more easily impressed colleges had called her.

Janice Thorton was a VIP amongst the VIPs, and owned the company that had designed and built the *Ark*. As Wendy approached the door to Thorton's apartment-sized accommodations she couldn't help but feel bemused to find it guarded.

"I'll have to scan you and check you for weapons—do you have any weapons, nurse?" smiled one of the guards lazily.

"I could easily kill with any number of these medical instruments," Wendy responded dryly.

The two guards laughed.

"You're clean, in you go," said the youngest.

Security was pretty lax aboard the *Ark*. Weapons and backgrounds had been screened before boarding, and the likelihood of any wrongdoing (considering their predicament) was pretty low. The door hissed open and the room on the other side was larger than the entirety of Wendy's shared dorm. In the centre of the room, on a couch that looked more comfortable than Wendy's bunk, relaxed *The* Janice Thorton.

"Come in dear, come in," she said cheerily.

Mrs Thorton was only a year older than Wendy, and appeared to be enjoying the glass of wine in her hand.

"How goes it—is the infection under control?" she gesticulated with her glass.

The infection was decidedly *not* under control, and Wendy was sure Mrs Thorton was perfectly aware of that matter.

"Data analysis is not my job. I'm just here to make the routine visits," Wendy replied simply.

Mrs Thorton did not seem entirely surprised by the response and the avoidance of the subject. She perhaps, Wendy thought, had (in her enjoyment of her wine) forgotten what she had asked in the first place.

"I'll need to swab your mouth," Wendy informed her.

"I built this ship, you know?" Mrs Thorton bragged.

"Yes," Wendy agreed.

"We don't know for sure that it will be better—you know, *in the future*," she confided in a whisper.

"I figured as much," responded Wendy.

"The passengers believe though, they believe in the *Ark*, in my ship," continued Thorton, though now she seemed distant, and the bragging had ended.

"They do," Wendy nodded, placing the swab into Thorton's mouth.

Wendy did not think that Mrs Thorton was lying to people when she told them of the possibility of a utopian future. Thorton had always been very good at hiring the right people and, when they had left Earth's standard time, most of Earth's best scientists and engineers (now on board the *Ark*) had been under her employment. She was the mastermind behind the masterminds of the operation. She had never understood the science, but she did understand the potential of the explanation of the science that her scientists had given her. As such, when Mrs Thorton confidently made statements such as "predictive algorithms have determined that, by the year 3137, the quality of life on Earth will have equalled or surpassed pre-plague states", Wendy could rest assured that, though neither she nor Thorton understood what a predictive algorithm was, it would no doubt have been implemented and studied by someone fully qualified to make such an evaluation.

"Mrh-hrh-pmgp!" continued Mrs Thorton.

"Yes indeed," agreed Wendy.

The swab turned blue, Wendy administered the needle, and Thorton took another sip.

In the mess hall Wendy sat to choke down her evening's food rations. Next to her sat a chef who had minutes before prepared a three-course meal that he was not permitted to enjoy, and was instead eating vitamin supplements from a food synthesiser.

"I came for two reasons and two reasons only. One, I love adventure, and two, because I love not dying!" he laughed.

"Not me," replied a doctor sternly.

"Oh?" said the chef surprised, "You're not a fan of adventure and survival?" he added.

"Of course not!" said the doctor. "I'm here for the month's pay," he chuckled, and was met with a good amount of laughter from those around.

"Doc, isn't it more likely we get the virus in here, you know, all crammed together like this?" asked a guard.

"Sure it is, but we had a pretty good chance of getting it on Earth anyway," replied the doctor.

"Besides," another guard chimed in, "that Thorton woman seems to think there will be a cure when we get out, so it doesn't matter if we get it anyway," he added.

"Just like we cured the common cold," quipped a member of the nursing staff, to which some medical staff laughed, and others looked worried.

"How's that?" asked the first guard.

"We didn't," responded the doctor.

"Oh well," responded a member of the cleaning staff as he sat down next to Wendy, "I don't mind if they still haven't cured the cold in the future, so long as they've got this plague under wraps," he concluded.

Wendy nodded and said nothing.

"And what about you, love; what do you hope the future holds?" he asked.

Wendy remembered when things had first begun to turn really bad. At first there were those that had downplayed what was going on, but the evidence stacked up, and quickly became undeniable. Her once full apartment building quickly became half full, and before long she was one of only a few residing there, then one of only a few on the street. Her city had been one of the worst hit, but none were passed over by the deadly disease. When talks of the *Ark* had first begun it was seen as a pipedream, and then it was made fun of, and then it was criticised as a waste of materials, and then it was built.

Some had tried to sell it as a safe haven for humanity. They argued that "even if humanity were to be wiped out from the plague, those aboard the *Ark* would still emerge from it in one thousand years to breathe life back into the planet". This line was still even being repeated by some on the week that Wendy had boarded. It was, of course, hogwash. The plague making its way onto the *Ark* was an almost certainty so if when they did emerge in a week's time there was still no cure, then those afflicted would die just as they would have done if they had caught the disease a thousand years earlier. It was—despite whatever those on board told others and themselves—not an endeavour that had been undertaken for altruistic reasons. The *Ark* had been built by billionaires who were here to avoid death and recession (and not necessarily in that order), and to them it was never about saving humanity.

But what did Wendy want? She would be lying to herself if she said she was doing this to help people. That *is* what she had first gone into nursing for—to help people—but that had been a long time ago. And it wasn't as though she couldn't have continued helping people on Earth, without having boarded the *Ark*. So what drove her now? Was it fear?

Fear that she herself may get the disease in a time with no cure and die? Had she come in hopes that, in the future, they might have found said cure?

Sure, that may be part of it, but Wendy thought there was more to it than that. It wasn't so much the prospect of a cure that thrilled Wendy, nor the proposed financial gains, but simply escaping the endless death and suffering that had been her life for the better part of half a decade.

The man had asked her what she hoped the future would hold, but Wendy wasn't really sure she had any real hopes for the future, beyond it being different from the past.

"Ow! That hurt!" yelped Andrew Stevensons.

Andrew Stevensons was another "*The* Andrew Stevensons" sort of guest. He was perhaps the wealthiest person on board, even (perhaps) more so than Mrs Thorton. He was also almost certainly the meanest.

"It's just a little prick," Wendy consoled.

"The principle hurts more than the needle," he replied.

"I didn't mean to jab you with principle," retorted Wendy.

"You know these drug synthesisers you doctor types use directly rip off the technology from my food synthesisers? Do you really think that it's fair that Thorton has to pay for my technology to be used on her ship, but your hospitals just steal it?" he grumbled.

"I wouldn't know anything about such things; I'm just the nurse," replied Wendy flatly.

Wendy in truth knew *all* about such things. Mr Stevensons had been a hot topic in hospitals over the last few years. When he discovered that his food synthesiser technology could be modified to create potentially life-saving drugs, he had asked for an exorbitant amount for their use. There wasn't a country in the world that wasn't close to bankruptcy (except for those that were already bankrupt), and so it was globally decided to simply violate his patent and start producing drug synthesisers without his permission. His constant unsuccessful attempts to sue hospitals and governments over this had often been featured on the news, and it was further speculated that, were his food synthesiser technology similarly violated, it would likely end world hunger. When Wendy considered all that Stevensons could have done, and all that he had instead chosen not to do, she found that the man sickened her deeply.

He's just a little prick, Wendy thought to herself as she left the room.

As the final week came to an end, many guests on board the *Ark* bitterly complained over how slowly the month had passed. Wendy felt the opposite, and figured any amongst the staff would too have felt it rushed by. With the increasing number of sick on board, her breaks had decreased in length and frequency, until it seemed the only time that she was not working were the few hours of sleep that she took by necessity. For a moment Wendy found herself reflecting on how strange it was that people could have such differing experiences of time, but caught herself and laughed at the notion, considering she was quite literally within a time-distorting bubble. Even so, with fifteen percent of those on board dying during the four-week period and another forty percent falling ill, all were relieved when finally the fourth week came to an end, and the *Ark* re-entered normal time.

Those that could still stand were gathered in a conference hall now too large for the diminished numbers of those left present. A stage stood in front of giant metal shutters that blocked the view of space from those within, and Mrs Thorton had taken the stand. She had grown thin and gaunt from her ongoing bout with the disease and seemed, as she spoke, to hold the podium in order to steady herself. Wendy barely listened, and instead watched with anticipation the sheets of heavy metal that would soon pull away to reveal their new home. There was applause, but it was extremely light. Thorton had just completed her speech about "new prospects and new horizons" or some such malarkey, and informed them that they would soon be boarding shuttles that would take them from the *Ark* to Earth. With the brief ceremony coming to an end, they now stood waiting for the *Ark*'s protective shutters to open and reveal their future home.

How much had changed became immediately evident when, with shutters opened, those on board quickly found that they were just one of many unnatural celestial bodies hanging above the planet. A planet that itself had noticeably changed in their absence, its forests looking greener and larger, its oceans looking bluer, and for a moment there was hope.

Then a crackling came over the loudspeakers within the *Ark*'s conference room, followed by a voice that spoke English in an unfamiliar accent:

"Traitors of the Plague-Commune *Ark*, this is Captain Jones of the Sol Ship *Veras*. No-one is to leave your vessel until the disease you carry on board has been terminated."

Silence fell across the deck, and someone behind Wendy mouthed the word "traitor" in disbelief. They would later learn that the cure had been discovered a mere two years after their leaving, but the road back to prosperity had been a long one. With most prominent doctors, scientists, and engineers aboard the *Ark*, there were few left who were well equipped to help rebuild society.

Thorton—visibly paled—thumbed on her broadcaster, hoping that it was still something that modern man knew how to receive.

"*Veras*, this is Janice Thorton of the *Ark*. We are refugees fleeing from a period of plague... we have sick—" she began.

The static and the crackling cut back in, and the voice interrupted.

"We do not recognise that term. *Refugees* look to escape to a separate, safer community, they do not isolate themselves from a community with the intention of returning to it and directly benefiting and *profiteering* from the very same society they abandoned to ruin," responded Captain Jones with clear anger.

"It was never our intention—" began Thorton weakly.

"Make your appeals to the council and the courts, *Ark*, but I warn you—as our ancestors that *you* abandoned suffered and died—we have had a thousand years to consider your actions."

"The courts..." she said quietly. "With what exactly are we being charged?" she asked.

"You are all charged with inhumane abandonment. Both of your own societies specifically, and humanity itself generally," came the response.

Wendy listened to the exchange with building horror.

Had it truly been so wrong of them to have abandoned the Earth of their past in search of a better life in Earth's future? Had she really had an obligation to stay and suffer? How many dead, and how much suffering, were they required to endure? Was it merely because they had left, or because they had left with the intention to return that they had transgressed? Would it have been different if they hadn't taken so many necessary scientists and doctors, or not expected to return to wealth?

Wendy wasn't certain on any of these points, but found it difficult to deny the sense of guilt she felt growing within her as the imposing shape of Sol Ship *Veras* moved between the *Ark* and the planet, obscuring Earth from their view.

An Earth that for a millennium had suffered and toiled and looked to the stars to see the *Ark* as symbolic of their suffering.

An Earth now angry and resentful.

The voice crackled back over the loudspeaker once more.

"You must now all answer your debt to humanity," it declared.

VOYAGE OF THE NETHAKRIN

Lightning lanced past the middle mast, briefly illuminating the black sails and swaying crow's nest of the besieged *Nethakrin*. Mr Trip, from his lofty crow's nest, battered by winds, hail, and sea spray, felt his hair stand on end, smelt burnt ozone, and tasted fear. They had entered the storm as a means to escape, and yet, upon entry, had found themselves eternally trapped.

The *Nethakrin*, dark and powerful, a three-masted tall ship formerly in the service of the King's Navy—a service that had abruptly ended when her captain and all loyal to him had been sent overboard at the point of pistol. It had been for no specific cargo that the ship's new master, Captain Bowden Forest, had led the mutiny, but for the ship itself. With heavy cannons, strong masts, and a name already known to both the lawful and lawless, the *Nethakrin* would make a fine and formidable pirate vessel.

Though they entered their new occupation with high hopes, bad luck soon followed. After only a short but successful run of piracy, a disastrous engagement with two vessels of the Spanish Navy resulted in loss of life and significant damage to the ship, forcing the *Nethakrin* and her crew to retreat into English waters. As they were piloting a vessel formerly belonging to the King's Navy, their time within these waters was tense. All able-bodied seamen not already engaged in repairs were on lookout, and Mr Trip was not to leave his lofty post for several days on end. Soon it was not merely the English that would spur their agitation, as even nature herself seemed to conspire against them. There were strong winds and heavy rains, and a growing darkness to the east.

It was the blackness of a storm that, once descended, carved a distinct line of bleak foreboding through the otherwise calm waters. It was as a drawn curtain, or funerary veil that revealed nothing beyond its threshold. They had seen many storms before, but with blue skies and calm waters to their north, south, and west, they had never before seen a storm such as the one now growing to their east. A storm of blackness so complete, and yet so contained.

For two days the *Nethakrin* skirted the storm, wary of its danger yet, due to her situation, not free to leave it behind. On the third day of his watch Mr Trip rubbed his eyes in hopes that they were playing tricks on him and, once assured that they were not, he alerted those below of his sighting. The sails he spied were still far off and on the horizon, the speck of a ship below them only just coming into view. Despite this, Mr Trip was sure that what he saw strongly and unsettlingly resembled that of the flagship of the King's Navy. Captain Forest did not bother to second-guess his man in the crow's nest. He knew that Mr Trip's eyes had never failed the *Nethakrin* before. Were she not to have suffered damage from the Spaniards, and were she to still have a full crew, even the flagship of the King's Navy would not have been capable of capturing the *Nethakrin*. However, damaged as she was, even with such a vast distance as her head start, there would be no outrunning their foe, and there would certainly be no outgunning her. It was with this sullen realisation (though broadcast as unquestioned confidence) that Captain Forest ordered his crew eastwards, commanding them to steer the *Nethakrin* directly into the black veil of the raging storm.

"The gallows or the storm," Captain Forest had put to them in a bellow, though he was not in fact offering a democratic choice. Her sails were reefed—there would be no steering against winds such as these—and the *Nethakrin* was left to the mercy of the storm. Upon entry the captain had hoped to ride out the weather, wait for it to pass or dissipate, and find themselves free and clear of their pursuer on the other side. He was not naive to the danger into which they entered; in fact, he was depending on it—hoping that their opponent would not be fool enough to follow, and figuring that their chances in the storm were better (though only marginally) than they were against their pursuer. If it worked it would mean continued freedom, and would hopefully only demand minimal repairs of their ship; however, mere moments into entering the cyclonic winds and apocalyptic thunder that lay beyond the black wall of clouds, the captain quietly lowered his expectations and simply hoped to die painlessly.

Days passed, and the storm that raged and tossed the *Nethakrin* showed no signs of relenting. Several members of the crew had disappeared since entry. They were presumed to have been swept overboard, though none had witnessed it happen. One seaman, unable to take the endless tossing, rain and thunder, had gone over intentionally. This *had* been witnessed, and it was reported that he had apologised to the former captain on his way down towards the sharp rocklike waves below. Morale was understandably low, and while only one man criticised the captain directly (and received a lead shot to the face for his trouble), whispers in the bunks and the mess, or yelled loudly in the privacy of the storm's roar, echoed the dead man's sentiment. They spoke of Captain Forest's looming incompetence, they spoke of regret and of a newfound appreciation for their former captain, and sometimes, with growing frequency, they even spoke of mutiny.

They also spoke of ghosts, spectres, and *the bell.*

There was no light in the storm but that which they shone from their own ship's ineffectually dull lanterns, and that which came with frequent thunder. Between the flashes, there was visibility of neither sea nor heaven. No sight of stars, and no testament to the waves beyond their spray and crash. Day was no different to night, and night no different to day; yet, despite this, those aboard the *Nethakrin* never lost track of time. They could not have done so, even if they had intended to. There was, from somewhere in the void, the chiming of a bell. An unseen bell that though inexplicable in existence marked (without fail) each hour of the day's progression with its haunting chimes. It chimed the hour, on the hour. It was heard to ring out sometimes nearby, and sometimes in the distance, yet never faltered or failed to meet its mark.

The exact location of the *Nethakrin* and her crew (lacking stars or any sense of control) was, beyond the vagary of their being somewhere in the Celtic Sea, impossible to determine. Despite this the captain and crew were perfectly aware that, whatever their exact location was, they were undoubtedly too far from land to explain the chime of any bell. They were near no large landmasses nor islands, so the haunting tones could not belong to a lighthouse, and neither lighthouses' nor ships' bells mark the hour in a fashion such as this bell did regardless.

Soon however, fear of the bell was met with further, more pressing concerns—a battering against the bottom of their ship. It started as a light tapping, escalated to a loud banging, and on occasion sounded as though it were the pounding of heavy canons and, as foreboding as the ghost chimes of a phantom bell were, the crew were increasingly more concerned by whatever it could be—in waters too deep for reefs and too far off for rocks—that battered again the *Nethakrin*'s underside with violent shunts and jarring bumps.

When first encountering these anomalies, crewmen began to assert (though none fully believed) that they had in fact (despite all logic to the contrary) run against uncharted reefs or rocks. If this were the case, there would be no avoiding them, and they would surely be wrecked. The bumps continued, but the *Nethakrin* remained unsunk, and Captain Forest suggested excitedly that perhaps the King's flagship *had* been fool enough to follow them, and that it was against her debris they now collided. Despite his wishful thinking, in the dark, it was all mere conjecture. Neither rock, nor reef, nor debris were ever seen and, between brief lightning flashes, even the sea itself remained invisible. While those few amongst the crew who still maintained any form of practicality continued to voice worries and fears that these impacts may wreck the *Nethakrin*, a growing number of seamen who stared in fear at the unseen churning void below began new whispers of what lightning revealed and postulated even stranger theories about against which they may be colliding.

Many of these theories went beyond any form of rationality. Concerned for their mortal lives, the crew who voiced them claimed that the mysterious clashes against the ship's keel were the knocks of the undead. The bumps, these seamen would say, were those crewmen against whom they had mutinied, knocking on the bottom of the ship, long cold and long dead yet wishing to be rescued from the churning black. It was these superstitious men who too claimed that the bell chimes carried on the winds belonged not to an unseen structure or ship, but instead were also of the dead. They were, they whispered, the waterlogged screams of the damned.

Others told stranger stories still. They spoke of a town, village, or city that sat below them, sunken and moss covered, and occasionally illuminated by lightning strikes before being quickly obscured once more by ferocious waves. It was, these crewmen claimed, not the knocking of lost souls that disturbed the bottom of their ship, but the roofs of long-abandoned buildings and the tops of tall trees in a vast sunken forest. The bell, these crewmen theorised, likely belonged to the church of the town below.

These theories were, the captain claimed, all superstitious hogwash.

The captain reasoned that if even Mr Trip from the crow's nest was unable to make out anything ahead of them from above water, no-one could possibly have any chance of making out any objects below. It was, the captain insisted, mere superstitious delusion that anyone thought they had sighted any such structures on the ocean floor, and he further did not see fit to so much as address the claims of the undead come knocking. Even so, regardless that none could agree on the cause, it was indisputably clear that there was *something* against which the *Nethakrin* knocked, and that each hour, from *somewhere*, a bell did chime to mark its passing.

The captain, unswayed by the knowledge that ships' bells do not chime to mark the hour, feared that the bell belonged to another vessel—unseen in the blackness. It was due to this fear that, despite the dangerous winds and lightning, Mr Trip (under orders) remained in the crow's nest. Mr Trip, with visibility so poor, saw little point in the matter, but was unwilling to join his fellow crewmates who had preceded him in disobedience to death. Even if he, and those aboard the *Nethakrin* were to learn of the owner of the bell, it was unclear to Mr Trip what exactly the captain intended to do. Whether it belonged to a ship, a lighthouse, the crew's supposed church or the screams of the dead, the fact remained that they themselves had neither manoeuvrability nor control, and were entirely at the mercy of the winds. Whatever the case, "remain in the crow's nest" Mr Trip did, and while visibility was non-existent, it soon became apparent from volume alone that to whatever the bell belonged, they and it were apparently moving closer together.

When the bell chimed four times to mark 4 am it was still in the distance, scarcely heard over the howling winds, but by the fifth bell of 5 am one could believe that, were it not for the dark sightlessness by which they were obscured, the lighthouse or ship would be within spitting distance. With reefed sails, this increased closeness was, of course, by no effort of the crew. Even so, closer they drew, and those amongst the crew who postulated superstitious theories began to suggest that their increased proximity was perhaps not entirely without reason, aim, or intent. Captain Forest once more disputed these claims, though without conviction, as he paced as best he could back and forth across the twisting and slanting deck. The agitation, or perhaps the stress, of command within such circumstances was clearly shown upon his pale haggard face as he mumbled counterarguments of "pure superstition" and "utter hogwash" towards no-one and nothing in partic- ular. It was almost time for the bell to strike six before the captain's pacing was ceased suddenly by the shout from the crow's nest: "Ahoy, land!"

With visibility so low, Mr Trip, despite his elevation, saw it only moments before the rest. But, once sighted, like step- ping through a door from a storm into a warm home, the *Nethakrin* and her crew were suddenly in calmer waters that stirred and frothed, but tossed no more.

Behind and around them the storm still raged. They were at the inside edge of a vast circular wall of black clouds that tapered upwards, impenetrable to the eye's gaze, and out of which they had just exited. In the very centre of the circle sat a small low island, and atop it a tall dark structure. While they were still a sensible distance from landfall, the risk of danger was immanent, as the ocean floor quickly shallowed and rose upwards to meet the small island. Fearing they may run aground, they immediately dropped anchor, and under orders from the captain began to ready the *Nethakrin*'s two longboats.

Despite the calmer waters and the minuscule circle of blue sky that shone through the small hole where the concave storm walls almost met, the crew, as they rowed out of the white froth towards the island, quickly found themselves immensely unsettled. No longer could the captain claim "total hogwash" against his crew's superstitious theories.

The waters of the beach nearing the small rocky island were crystal clear, and below them, equally clear, was the view of a vast village, spanning far into the distance, and far beyond where the dark wall and heavy waves obscured it. How far it spread none could say for certain, nor could they claim with certainty whether it had actually been against roofs and trees that the *Nethakrin* had been colliding, but with many crewmen giving voice to how wrong the captain had been, Captain Forest was glad that he had ordered the entire crew onto the longboats and towards the island and its dark structure, and left none aboard his ship unsupervised.

The structure rose out of the ocean on a rocky base that stood only five metres above the waves, an island only large enough to contain it, and it alone: *it, the structure, the Black Cathedral.*

The crew beached their boats as best they could against the nearly non-existent shoreline, and quickly tied them off against the rusted remnants of a black fence. The structure was of a magnificent design that invoked memories of the Gothic style, but appeared perhaps far, far older. Moss covered and engraved with strange script, both the Black Cathedral and its island appeared beyond ancient. Gargoyles flanked the entrance to the structure's large wooden doors, and crouched peering down ominously from outcroppings all over its tall walls. From the vantage point of the shore the crew could now see that the island had once, perhaps, not been an island at all, but instead a hill. There was, running from the submerged village below, a long winding path that ran up the sunken hill and exited the shore to meet the small island on which they now stood. The size of the cathedral was staggering. It rose high above them, and if their tall ship had been stacked upon itself twice over the masts would perhaps only just reach the top of the structure's lofty bell-tower—a belltower of dark granite only backlit enough by the lightning of the storm to be sighted, and through those lightning flashes it was whispered by the crew that the tower had no bell.

All hesitated before the dark strucutre, then two of the captain's few trusted crewmen were ordered to stay with the longboats, while the rest were ordered inside. As they passed through the cathedral's doors, some whispered that it stood as worse than a bad omen. Others, the captain amongst them, felt the cathedral to be a good sign, pointing out that it seemed that the church was holding back the dark storm's walls, rather than causing them. Regardless, it was not open to debate. Fearing a mutiny, the captain permitted *only* those two so ordered to guard the boats to remain outside. There was, in fact, little enough room for the crew to stand outside anyway, even if they had wanted to, but still it took the captain's order of "Inside, you dogs!" to get many of the more superstitious members to move beyond the tall rotting doors of warped oak, and beyond the outer gargoyles which seemed to howl with winds of their own.

As they entered, Captain Forest made sure to keep an ear out, and carefully noted who amongst his crew mumbled with the most discontent. None of the crew nor the captain had rested well since entering the storm a week prior, and all of them, despite being experienced sailors, stumbled and wobbled on legs unaccustomed to the stable, unmoving nature of land. The cathedral's interior was dark and damp. Molluscs grew high up on the temple's pillars, seaweed hung from the pews, and a scattering of scampering crabs and dead fish littered the floor, all attesting to the fact that this cathedral, much like the town beneath it, was too once submerged. Inside, the crew quickly learned that they were not alone. In the centre of the cathedral's vast cavernous room, kneeling before an idol, were three men seemingly absorbed in prayer.

All present stood frozen in stunned shock until finally the captain approached the worshippers. He could hear Mr Trip mutter behind him, and several others murmured quietly in agreement. It was however, now not of mutiny that they whispered, but instead exclusively of ghosts and monsters.

Reaching the three kneeling men, the captain corrected the superstitious assessment, stating "No, not ghosts; just dead."

It was difficult to tell how long the three men had been dead. They were, it seemed, not quite skeletal, with what appeared to be dark, rotten flesh still clinging to their bones. They had no hair, no facial features, and in some parts of their body their flesh was, on closer inspection, not of man, but seaweed and mud from the ocean floor. Whether they had fully decomposed and were now covered by deceptive sea stuff, or if the ocean had in some way preserved some of their humanity, was of little real importance. What was clear was clear regardless. They were dead, and in death had seemingly continued their silent prayer to the strange idol for countless centuries.

After discovering this the captain dispatched groups of men to search the area, making sure to include amongst each group's ranks men he felt he could still somewhat trust. One group was to remain and search the cathedral's main room, another to descend into the catacombs in search of funerary riches, and the last to ascend the belltower in search of anything of worth. As they went off, the captain stayed to examine the strange golden idol that had remained the focus of the worshippers even in death. It seemed to be of solid gold, and while not of distinctly Christian iconography, was vaguely suggestive of it. Unfortunately, as the three groups returned, it became increasingly apparent that the idol was perhaps the only thing of worth available to them within the ancient structure. Those who had searched the main room reported that most decorations had been tainted with rust, or decomposed too completely to be identifiable, let alone to be of any worth. Those who had attempted the catacombs below found them unsurprisingly flooded, the riches within (if any) entirely inaccessible. It was, however, not until the group from the tower returned that the captain had gone from dismay to anger, with the crewmen reporting that not only was there nothing of worth, but also that there had been no bell.

It was this claim, this lack of a bell, that had angered the captain. He held that his head was level, and having heard the bell, believed it must exist. He further believed that there was no other place from which its chime could have possibly rung out. Immediately ordering two men to accompany him, Captain Forest began climbing the tower himself. It was a difficult climb, as the tower, much like the rest of the cathedral, was in serious disrepair. However, after many hundreds of slippery steps of rotten wood, the captain found himself at the tower's summit, with a view of the submerged town below and raging storm beyond. There was no bell, that much the captain was ready to concede. However, before they began the long descent from the Black Cathedral's tall tower, the hour became 7 am, and was marked by the seven ghostly chimes of an unseen bell, which vibrated out from the absence in which no bell hung.

Impossibly, the phantom bell rang out, and chimed seven times with the steady hand of a metronome. It chimed, and in the ocean's stillness the forgotten village long submerged sprang to life. The bell chimed and rotted doors swung open, and mud men, women, and children of seaweed and grot like those three who worshipped below began to exit their homes. It chimed and these damned creatures of the depths began their silent vigil up the winding path, up and out of the tides, climbing their way towards the once submerged Black Cathedral.

With considerably more speed than they had ascended, the captain and his two men found themselves back on ground level, looking out from the structure's far end towards the large rot-wood doors and beyond to the sea. The long-dead parishioners of the doomed sunken city marched from the water's calmness in slow procession towards the doors and past the gargoyles and into the Black Cathedral. They filed silently into the main room, and took their places amongst the rot-wood pews.

Many of the crew stood, looking in pale silent horror as these creatures of muck and rank moved amongst them. Those crewmen who were stunned were not the captain's immediate concern, however. Some men were missing, and the strange golden idol had gone with them. Captain Forest was not too concerned by the lack of an idol, but by those who had taken it. It wasn't the loss of golden riches that worried him. At this point in his failed venture not making a profit was a foregone conclusion. However, with the idol gone, and some crew unaccounted for, the captain, with renewed fear, believed a mutiny had already taken place, and worried that he had been betrayed, abandoned, and left marooned on this small island surrounded by strange devils.

There was no doubt in the captain's mind that those missing had retreated towards the longboats and, without him, cast off, abandoning him and the island for the *Nethakrin*.

He had left two good men with the boats, but doubted any amongst his crew, even his most trusted and level-headed men, were brave or loyal enough to not lose their spines when confronted with such unholy monstrosities.

The captain was in a frenzy and, snapping those amongst him into action, ordered that they now must make for the longboats, and in doing so be careful to avoid any contact with the strange faceless dead.

The first boat had indeed been taken, and the captain clambered into the second, vowing to send back the first for those that did not fit, though never truly intending to do so.

The waters surrounding the temple had ceased to be calm, and within the temple the strange congregation could be heard to moan in loud mournful inhuman cries.

The winds and the rains and the thunder penetrated the surrounding wall of darkness, which began to collapse and encroach inwards, and lightning struck even amongst the Black Cathedral's tall tower, and snarling gargoyles.

The congregation within the Black Cathedral moaned louder and with increased grief, while sight of the *Nethakrin* and the longboat ahead was periodically lost behind tall waves of growing magnitude as their longboat was lifted and dropped and lifted again.

The waves tossed them and turned them, and the mud men moaned, and the traitorous longboat ahead was capsized and sent below to the quiet village of the faceless damned.

The creatures moaned, and lightning struck the crow's nest of the *Nethakrin*, splitting her main mast in two, and setting her sails aflame.

They moaned, and the *Nethakrin* was sighted turned on her side by the great waves, then quickly pulled below, broken, claimed by the unrelenting storm.

They moaned and the captain and his men were given no other option but to turn back, to seek shelter and sanctuary once more in the Black Cathedral that even now the ocean had begun to reclaim.

To seek sanctuary.

To join the faceless damned amongst the rotted pews.

And to worship forevermore, below, the unseen bell.

A BOOK OF TRUTH

Book of Truth, or Truth. ⅕ STARS.

I speed read it cover to cover, and all I got out of the experience was the book store's loyalty points and a mild headache. The only reason I have given this book one star is because ReviewBooks does not allow you to rate zero.

Nathan Zackman, 12/3/2048

When Sergeant Harry Donovan entered the room he found it empty, save for the deserted benches and the book that stood upon a simple lectern. Approaching the stand he could see that the book was opened to page one. It was not numbered and Harry knew that no pages within the book would be. Harry knew this book well. It was opened to a title page that he had seen reproduced in many places before. Blank—albeit for one word: "Truth". This was the *Book of Truth*, and the room within which he stood had belonged to the New Terran Seekers of Universal Truths. They were no doubt all dead now, from poison, or some other self-inflicted death. Their bodies were likely in one of the many rooms that made up the factory grounds, though none had yet been discovered. They may not be discovered. They may have perished in the factory's furnaces, or they may have thrown themselves into the raging open sewage lines that ran beneath the structure. Their clergy had numbered roughly three hundred, so their demise could conceivably have been a mixture of all three. Whatever the case may be, none of the officers that were currently scouring the grounds of the large factory really expected to find anyone still alive.

All this over a simple book, Harry thought, closing it, and turning it over in his hands. It was the hardcover edition, retailing at forty-five dollars. He had seen countless copies of this book over the last few years—on the news, in magazines, and as a constant fixture in the window of the small bookstore he passed on the way to the station each morning. On more than one occasion copies of it had wound up in police evidence lock-up. The cover was a dark crimson with a faux-leather feel to it. There was no blurb on the back, no title on the front, and no author listed. Despite this, Sergeant Harry Donovan recognised it all the same, it was, if anything, distinct in its nondescriptness. The book was the *Book of Truth*, and the author was the infamous madman, Gasop Trot.

Truth, long before its release, was guaranteed to become a bestseller in the same way that any strange and forbidden curiosity was. Written in jail by the convicted leader of a suicide cult, and published posthumously from his scribbled raw manuscript, *Truth* was advertised to the public as the devil-ramblings of a most notorious madman. It was conjectured by some that he had written it in blood on his cell's walls. Harry knew for a fact that this was false, and that Gasop had been provided a pencil and a legal pad to write on during his incarceration. He also strongly suspected that the rumours had been started by the publication's advertising house, though he wasn't sure it had really been necessary.

There was—in Harry's experience—nothing that interested the supposedly sane public more than the mind of a madman, and Gasop was as mad as they came. People are always drawn to the grisly and the terrible and the strange and the sad, and so, just as when in 2016 the lifting of the ban on *Mein Kampf* saw it become a bestseller in Germany, so too did *Truth* on release quickly become the smash-hit bestseller in the summer of 2047.

The controversial sale of his book was by no means the first time Gasop had found himself in the public eye. There had been, in his early days, protests outside churches and universities alike. What exactly he was protesting was never clear, though he had seemed to offer an underlying criticism of the institutes supposedly peddling lies and hypocrisies. These protests were small, rarely covered by the media, and built only a very small handful of followers. This changed in 2039 when he and his followers had burned down a church, resulting in his first arrest and his first taste for international news coverage.

"If you want to make the news, then burn down a church," he was later famously quoted as having advised.

To the media, Gasop was the golden goose. They widely covered his arrest, trial, and subsequent release. Following this, whenever they were faced with a slow news day or empty bulletin, they were more than happy to broadcast and admonish him on any opinion he had on any matter. The relationship was largely symbiotic. The media received their ratings, and Gasop gained his followers.

Harry laid the book back down on the lectern, reopened it, and began to scan his eyes over the words. He had heard and seen quotes from the book before, but had never actually read from it directly. It took a few seconds of reading before Harry began to realise that the sentences had a strange appearance of saying *something*, but what exactly it was that they said was never quite clear. He found himself reading a paragraph and only upon reaching its end noticing that he had, despite taking in each word individually, grasped no larger understanding of what it had meant. Harry's fellow officers, as he himself should have been doing, were going through the rooms, double-checking and triple-checking them for the missing clergy. As his radio intermittently rattled off their updates, Harry turned another unnumbered page and strained his brows attempting to get anything out of the strange writings of Gasop Trot.

It appeared to Harry to be largely incoherent, but, on reflection, being largely incoherent was by no means the worst, or most critical, review *Truth* had ever received. Shortly following, and even preceding, its release *Truth* was immediately slammed by both church and parent groups for inciting violence and promoting Satanism, and the book quickly found itself banned from the domains of both institutions. However, these claims were based more on the book's author than on the merits of the book itself, and in reality were largely unfounded. In truth, due to the vague and indiscernible nature of Gasop's writing, it would be difficult to point to any specific passage that could credibly be said to opt for any particular doctrine whatsoever. Despite this, there was a small, but concerning, number of people who *did* claim to have found meaning within its writings, and they lauded the text as gospel on the streets to uninitiated pedestrians. Most who heard these preachers felt they were doing no more than spouting vagaries. Some scholars would go on to theorise that the text was, in a sense, a written version of a Rorschach test, and that those finding either controversy or meaning in it were, in actuality, simply imposing their own beliefs upon a splattering of total gibberish.

Controversial as the text may have been, it was, however, by no means a controversial fact that in the year 2045 Gasop Trot led his somewhat campily named cult, The Terran Seekers of Universal Truth, in an act of group suicide that saw 39 people dead, 112 hospitalised, and Gasop himself jailed for murder, inciting suicide, kidnapping, and child endangerment. Nor was it an uncontroversial fact that, even before the posthumous publication of the book, those who followed Gasop's teachings appeared to subscribe to a belief system entirely alien to outsiders. There was, following his cult's mass suicide, a lengthy investigation, which included (but was not limited to) interviews with survivors, and with Gasop himself. The findings were entirely inconclusive. Despite the extensive investigation no coherent public understanding of the cult's doctrines could be grasped. It wasn't that Gasop was not willing to talk about the doctrines, but instead that—much like his later writings—what he said was, to most people, entirely incomprehensible.

Harry could not help but think of that investigation, and those interviews now, as he blinked at the words that blurred in front of him. The police radio chatter was an unheard background ambience. Harry was finding that as he read his mind wandered and, despite his eyes flickering over every word and his lips lightly mouthing them, daydreams drew his attention to the true absurdity of the case he was on.

Due to a tip-off, Harry and his team had surrounded the facility, and engaged in a three-day siege with the occupants—the "New Terran Seekers of Universal Truths". Despite Gasop being dead, and the new clergy having no previous members, the adoption of the name had led to fears of a similar pending mass-suicide. When those within the factory's walls had suddenly ceased any form of communication with the police negotiators outside, they had raided it, hoping to save all they could, only to find it empty. It wasn't corpse filled like they had expected, but genuinely abandoned.

The rooms that Harry had seen when first searching the premises were impressive. The clergy could have continued to survive the siege for months if they had wished to. There was canned food, bottled water, medicines and even toilet paper heavily stockpiled, yet within each room they searched no sign of life could be found. The search had continued and grown more thorough, and eventually led to Harry discovering the factory's makeshift church house, and the open book.

And now here he stood.

With effort Harry brought himself back to the present. He was finding that it was nearly impossible to not have his mind wander as he read the book, and he was now finding it difficult to recall anything that he had so far been reading. He appeared to be roughly eighty pages in, and (being that he was a slow reader) he was shocked to find that he had read so much. However, his mind had wandered the whole time, and though he had read the pages, he wasn't sure how much—if anything—he had taken in of the strange ramblings.

Harry strained his memory. From what he could recall of what he had been reading, it was a critique on some philosopher's argument, but he could not recall if the philosopher or the argument had ever been named. Harry turned back the page to see if he had missed it, and began reading forward again, only to find that the paragraphs were not rebutting a philosophical text, but instead appeared to be reviewing a poem, though once again the subject of the review was never directly mentioned. He could also not understand how this could possibly tie in to the talk of philosophy only one page over. Turning forwards again to the page he had just left, Harry found that it was discussing Newtonian physics, not philosophy. Had Harry been mistaken? *Could* he be so mistaken?

With a heavy-set frown and furrowed brow, Harry, despite himself, pushed on, turning back the pages again, and beginning once more from the first page, simply titled 'Truth'.

When the factory siege had begun, *Truth* had already been a bestseller for the better part of a year. Despite this, it was difficult to determine exactly how many people had actually read it, and read it thoroughly. There were plenty who had simply bought it because of the controversy it represented, like a thirteen-year-old watching an R-rated movie. Most had acquired it as a curiosity and having browsed the first few pages were content to leave it at that. Others had struggled further, decided it was nonsense, and left reviews to that effect. Some self-fashioned intellectuals talked of it being "visionary", "daring", and "breathtaking", and lauded it for its abandonment of narrative and form, though they admitted they could not read it all the way through. One reviewer referred to it as the "novelisation of a jazz scat solo", though left it to the reader to interpret whether this was a positive or negative.

There was, of course, the group who undeniably had read the book. A group that Harry was beginning to suspect, as he pawed over the text before him, were the only ones who had truly read it cover to cover, and had read it *closely*. This was the small but devoted group that began to form around the text, became the writing's most loudly spoken advocates, and would eventually form the New Terran Seekers of Universal Truths. It was often claimed by these readers that only *Truth* "truly sees", and they would boast it to be less contradictory or hypocritical than either the Christian bible or Anton LaVey's. Despite their lauding his book and having taken his cult's name, several members of the group were on record disregarding Gasop as a leader and prophet, claiming that he was instead an aerial, responsible for nothing more than relaying a message.

As 2048 waned the group had largely fallen out of the public interest. By the media they were noted as nothing more than a handful of eccentrics who had chosen to subscribe to and spout gibberish, while living in an abandoned factory in the town's industrial district. The police, however, paid them closer attention, noting that the group's members continued to swell in size and included the very young. When whispers and the tip-off of the ominously named but ever-vague "final truth" were picked up, Harry and his team were sent to prevent another occurrence of what had happened three years earlier.

And now here he was, and now here they weren't.

Harry was now almost towards the end of the book, and had become both fascinated by and fixated upon it. As he read, several dozen requests had crackled over the radio for him to check in, though his radio had now sat quiet for well over an hour. Harry should have responded, and he should not have dwelled in this room for so long—separated from the other officers—but found he could not tear himself away from the text. There was something about it that he could not place, accompanied by a growing certainty that he was drawing close to some form of understanding.

It wasn't merely for his own benefit that he read the text. If he understood *Truth*, and understood the madness that drove Gasop and his followers, then perhaps his insight could prevent this all from happening again. In his mind there was clearly *something* to the writings. There *had* to be. Harry was sure that so many people would not and could not have been swayed in such a similar way if there wasn't *something* to it, and as he read he slowly felt that he was beginning to discern what that something may be.

It reminded him of having had to study *A Clockwork Orange* in school; much like that book, this one had a language of its own that, as he read, he was beginning to understand. It was as though it was written in code, or perhaps operated in a logic that was entirely a thing of its own, and self-contained.

As he read, it all slowly began to form cohesively before him.

Nothing seemed clear on its first read-through, or even the second, or third, but Harry had now re-read many of these paragraphs many times over, and he was beginning to find clarity in their words. Clarity, and maybe even wisdom, and beauty.

Harry turned towards the final page, and as he read and re-read the words they rearranged before his eyes. They formed and reformed as new sentences, new words—strange answers to questions unasked and unknown conclusions.

He felt compelled, but compelled to what he could not say, and yet compelled all the same. There was something— something that he couldn't quite put his hands on but could see suspended just beyond his reach, and yet it approached.

All that was muddled was becoming not just apparent, but obvious, and eternally so, and as Harry came to the final line he realised that all that he had known prior, and all that preceded, now appeared to him as bafflingly dull, and absurdly misguided.

Suddenly the doors to the mock church swung open, and two officers entered the room. They scanned their torches across the empty benches, and settled them on Harry.

At some point, as he read, it had fallen dark, and Harry—the officers informed him—had not checked in for hours. He guessed that he had zoned out, or at least he told them that he guessed as much. Uneasily and shakily Harry closed the book before him, and walked towards his fellow officers, who were standing in the dull light of the doorway.

Back in the police station they were all debriefed.

Not one of the roughly three hundred clergy members had been found that evening, and their copy of the *Book of Truth* had been one of the few items from the factory to be entered into evidence.

Harry's lost hours and his multiple failures to check in had been reported, and he was given a week off for sick and stress leave.

On his way from the station back to his small apartment, Sergeant Harry Donovan passed the small bookstore that he went by every day on his way to work. In the window stood a hardcover copy of the *Book of Truth*, retailing for forty-five dollars.

Could his comprehension of this text really have prevented today's tragedy, or future tragedies?

Was it not his duty—even while on sick leave—to do what he could to prevent further such happenings?

Harry entered the store and readied his money.

He had only read from the book once, and yet felt that he had begun to understand it and its followers.

He had only read from it once, and yet felt that he was beginning to agree.

DEVIL IN THE GARAGE

Tobyn—dressed all in black—was standing in his small garage. The smell of paint was almost overwhelming. For a brief moment he considered opening the garage door for fresh air, but pushed away the thought, knowing darkness to be necessary.

Imagery was a big part of Satanic rituals—all of the texts that Tobyn had read had said so. He had felt silly drawing the pentagram in red spray paint—as though he was faking it, or something. But the "summoning" didn't necessarily require blood—which was good, as he didn't have any prepared. *No animals were harmed in the making of this Satanic ritual*, Tobyn thought, and chuckled. It seemed from his research that "looking the part", or *symbolism*, was in many respects just as powerful as the "real thing" and, considering his alternative to the red paint was a can of British racing green, Tobyn felt confident in his choice.

He crouched to light the candles. There were five, each standing at one point of the pentagram and smelling pleasantly of lilac—*perhaps another first in this kind of situation*—but black candles aren't easy to find, and Tobyn had taken what he could get.

It had been roughly one month since Tobyn had begun feverishly researching the black arts, and he had now reached a point in which he believed that he had not only learned what was required to summon a demon, but also what those summoned were driven by. He felt confident he knew by what rules demons and spirits lived, and were bound.

With each of the small black candles lit, Tobyn sat back, and considered that the last time he had lit a candle was while trying to woo a girl at a romantic dinner. Absurdly, he had been more nervous on that occasion. He reached back and grabbed his book.

A Book of Spells, Incarnations, Magik, and Evokations: the book had come pre-tattered with pages yellowed by ink to look as though they had been weathered by time. The book had been ordered online and in the section below the listing that stated "users who ordered this also bought" there had been books on crystals, feng shui and aromatherapy. The book was copyright 2006. Despite its newness, Tobyn's recently acquired book of spells had been heavily vetted— or at least as heavily vetted as such pseudoscience can be. A good number of self-proclaimed amateur witches and warlocks had given the book good reviews online, and it had a 4½-star rating on the ReviewBooks website. Initially it had seemed strange to Tobyn for a book of magic to be so new, and Tobyn had had to fight against a romanticised bias that required such things to have ancient origins. He'd had to reason and remind himself that even the Bible had been new once—so age should not be held against it, and that while the same publisher who handled this book also sold teen-romance novels, Tobyn noted that the Ouija Board is sold by Hasbro, and plenty still swear by *its* occult authenticity.

There were countless spells for endless things found within: desire spells, health spells, love spells—many requiring certain crystals, herbs, and "positive vibes". Tobyn turned past all of these to the big guns: "Evokations"—the heading was spelt like that, with a *k*, like the old-fashioned spelling of "magik", though the actual articles that followed used modern spelling throughout. Under "Evokations" Tobyn turned to "Demons".

Tobyn had never been much of a believer in magic—that was, until last month when his father, on his eightieth birthday, had been the sudden victim of spontaneous human combustion. This had surprised perhaps everyone *except* Tobyn's father, who had told Tobyn on multiple occasions that the good fortune he had received during his life was due to a pact with the devil. A pact that, his father had always claimed, would end on his eightieth birthday. While Tobyn at first had thought his father *actually* dying at that date to be a mere coincidence, he had slowly, over the last few weeks (largely due to his own rapidly declining health) decided he might now be willing to believe.

Tobyn could do with some luck right now. He had recently turned thirty years old. This was the same age that his older sister had been when she had died from cancer. She had warned him that her doctor had said it was likely hereditary, and that he had expressed surprise at the clean health their father had enjoyed. And now, with Tobyn experiencing extreme fatigue and aches similar to those which his sister had suffered, and awaiting test results that his doctor had warned were "not at all promising", Tobyn had begun to feel as though he were a wild animal with his back against the wall. Magic, Tobyn felt, was his best out.

If his father had truly avoided this family disease, and had enjoyed fifty years on the Devil's time, then it was *that* hereditary trait, not his sister's early death, that Tobyn intended to inherit. However, Tobyn had no intentions of spontaneously combusting, and so, going over his plan once more in his head, he ran his finger across the lines for "Demon Summoning", and began to stumble his way through the Latin words and ancient names.

"*Ave Satanis! Ave Satanis! Apophis, Lucifer, Loki, Lilith, Set, Beelzebub!*" Tobyn briefly wondered if all these guys knew each other, and had to fight back laughter.

More words, more Latin, more names, "*Ave Satanis!*" six times over, and darkness.

It seemed as though all light had been sucked from the room; then slowly the candles flickered back to life and within the centre of Tobyn's spray-painted pentagram crouched the creature.

The creature was dark dull red, horned, hooved, with forked tail and tongue. It was a demon—or the Devil himself—in appearance much as it was depicted in countless films and on countless band merchandise. Briefly Tobyn found himself wondering if popular culture had not desensitised him to such things, but then the creature spoke with the hiss of a snake and the rasp of a death rattle.

"Why have you called me?" it asked, or demanded.

"You speak English?" Tobyn said, surprised.

"Evidently. I am eternal," it responded with more than a hint of annoyance.

Tobyn sighed a breath of relief, and tossed aside his English-to-Latin dictionary.

"Good," he said.

The creature rose—and stood almost as high as the garage ceiling. The smell of sulphur and spray paint clashed for control, and the sulphur won out easily.

"Why have you summoned me?" asked the demon again, its annoyance turning to anger.

"Y-you grant wishes?" Tobyn quickly stuttered.

"Do I look like a genie, boy?!" The room grew hotter with its anger.

Tobyn had never seen a genie, so really wasn't sure, but elected not to inform the demon as much.

"I don't grant wishes; I make deals!" it roared, and Tobyn briefly wondered what the neighbours would make of all this noise.

"What is the price of these deals?" Tobyn asked.

"Only your immortal soul!" came the response.

"Oh." It was what Tobyn had expected. "Good."

"What is it you desire, human?" The creature leaned in, and its breath smelt of rancid meat.

"Well," began Tobyn, "there is this girl..." he lied.

The monster roared with laughter.

"Internal damnation for a *girl*? You humans never change!" it hollered.

"Do you think my terms cheat me?" Tobyn asked with as much surprise and earnestness as he could muster.

"It's your soul," said the demon indifferently.

Tobyn turned away as if to think, walked two thoughtful steps, and then turned back.

"What is a soul worth?" he enquired.

"More than a girl," came the laughed response.

"Riches?" asked Tobyn.

"Riches in life, in exchange for eternal hunger and wanting? Sure." It seemed much amused.

"And power?" Tobyn queried.

"Power in this world, for servitude in the next," agreed the demon.

"And what of long life and happiness?"

"Traded for an eternity of suffering," followed the demon.

"A soul is worth any of those?" Tobyn said with mock surprise.

"You creatures are narrowed by your perception; life on this plane is incomparable to what follows!" it boasted boomingly.

The creature was, in its arrogance and its desire to brag, showing much of its hand. Tobyn seemed like an easy mark, unsure of what he wanted, and yet certain he would willingly give his soul for it. The demon smiled and leaned in close again.

"Shall we deal?" it asked.

"It seems my soul is worth equal to, or more than, any one of these things offered," Toby said slowly, as if considering the offer.

The heat emitted from the demon intensified, causing Tobyn's eyes to water. Tobyn figured, and figured correctly, that it was a sign of the creature's anger. Demons need souls like man needs food—Tobyn had read as much in his research—and the way this demon was licking its lips, it seemed as though it could almost taste what Tobyn had to offer.

"Do not waste my time, human!" it thundered, and the flames from the candles rose to chest height.

Tobyn cowered appropriately at the show of power, then, acting bashful and awkward, began again: "It's just that I don't want... less than I could have... you know? May I... would I be able to have more than one thing you have offered me?"

Patience was a virtue, and so the demon lacked it. It stomped its feet and paced three steps in either direction within the small, painted pentagram. The worth of a human soul was great, and the creature was annoyed at Tobyn, but annoyed more so at itself for having revealed a portion of their worth to him. It was not encouraged to trade so much for a soul. Demons were supposed to get the best deals possible. But it also certainly wasn't forbidden to make a deal such as this, and the demon, feeling as though the soul was so close that it could touch it, was becoming desperate.

"Perhaps I could have both: the girl and the riches?" Tobyn tried.

"Yes, yes!" it cried in annoyance. A girl and money were still not much to give for a soul.

"Perhaps I could trade for three things?" Tobyn asked.

"Fine," it said, clearly vexed.

It was a lot to trade for one soul, but still a good deal. If anything, the demon just felt glad it would get the soul and be able to go back to Hell, and be free from dealing with this especially annoying human.

"Or... perhaps I might be able to trade my soul, for all of what you have offered?" Tobyn pushed.

"Yes, anything!" the demon cried in exasperation and excitement, the room growing hotter still.

"Deal," Tobyn said shortly.

"Deal," said the demon. It chuckled, and a smile spread across its face. "Your soul is mine, and for it you will receive—" it began to list what Tobyn had asked for.

"Oh, no," Tobyn cut in, "You said 'anything', and it is to that which we have just now agreed," he clarified, a smile of his own now spreading.

The creature's eyes narrowed, and the heat became of such intensity that the candles began to wilt and deform.

It *had* offered "anything", and the human had agreed. It was a binding contract.

"It is not wise to deceive a demon, boy," it warned.

"And yet, here we are," returned Tobyn with a laugh.

The creature was not amused.

"Your soul will still be mine in the end, so remember, as you make your request, that king as you might be here, I will make you pay for it tenfold in my domain!" it threatened.

"Noted," agreed Tobyn, unfazed.

He had steered the conversation to this point. His study had taught him what demons were, and were not, allowed to do. This was the chance he had been looking for.

"I want every human on the planet to instantly and irrevocably die in oh—", he referred to his wristwatch, "—three minutes time."

The demon's eyes shot wide open.

"What? Why?! *Every human*?! You will die too, mortal!" it raved.

"I'm aware, and the what and the why is my own business," Tobyn said calmly. "Boy, I bet all humans being dead will make winning their souls tough," he added in a mocking tone.

The demon felt anger, but also panic. Not only was this an embarrassment and an insult to its abilities, but—as the human had so annoyingly pointed out—it would also have far-reaching consequences beyond the fall of mankind. Executing this deal would not only end humanity, but so too would it end the supposedly eternal struggle for souls. There would be no-one left to be won to the light or to the dark, and Heaven and Hell would hunger and starve. The creature knew that this would be its own end as much as it was the human's. Worse yet, it would be at fault—it hadn't been careful in its dealings. Despite the threats that the creature had levelled against Tobyn for his trickery, in this deal it was the demon that would be punished, both by its own kind, and (no doubt) by the angels. Further, they—the light-borne—would likely not be content with punishing the responsible demon alone, and would surely level punitive measures against all of demon-kind. This action may well throw Heaven and Hell back into true conflict, *the apocalyptic kind*, a conflict for which the creature would be blamed, and yet... it was under contract. A contract that the demon could not break regardless of how desperately it wanted to. The creature would have no choice but to destroy humanity once three minutes had run their course, and in doing so it would be the instrument of its own destruction.

"I-I can't..." it stammered, and if a demon could turn pale, it would have.

"We have a deal, and the time is ticking," replied Tobyn.

"You would ask that all your kind die? Why?"

"Not *would ask; have asked*. And *why* is not your concern."

The creature paced, this time in agitation and fear, not anger and impatience. The room had grown cooler, and the candles were no longer melting.

"Although..." Tobyn began, as though he had just had a thought.

The demon whirled to face him.

"Although?" it repeated.

"We could perhaps trade," offered Tobyn. "Make a deal, you know?" he clarified.

"Yes?" asked the demon cautiously.

"A lifetime of eternal good luck. I would like a lifetime of eternal good luck," he outlined.

The demon straightened, and warmth slowly returned to the room.

"I get your soul... and you get eternal good luck?" the demon questioned.

"Oh no, no; that wouldn't do—as per our agreement you *have* my soul—it isn't mine to offer," Tobyn pointed out.

"Then what?" spat the demon, confused.

"You grant me eternal good luck, and I agree to let you out of our previous agreement. I would therefore keep my soul, and you wouldn't have to genocide a species," Tobyn clarified.

The intense heat returned.

"You expect me to give you this, for nothing in return?!" it roared.

"If not, you have thirty seconds to fulfil our previous deal," Tobyn said, calmly regarding his watch once more.

The demon roared. A bright flash and the smell of gunpowder filled the room. And then the demon was gone.

The candles were cold melted puddles on the floor, and the room quickly returned to the temperature it had been before the invocations had been cast.

Tobyn held his breath and watched the tick of the second hand—only fifteen seconds remaining.

As the seconds ticked by he could feel his fatigue subside, and his ache decline—but refused to accept it as anything more than the placebo effect.

There were five seconds left, and the home phone began to ring inside.

With any luck it would be his doctor calling with good news, and clean test results.

Three seconds left, and the phone was still ringing.

Tobyn felt better than he had ever felt before, but until time ran out he couldn't be certain that he hadn't doomed the entire human race to non-existence.

Two seconds left—he closed his eyes and crossed his fingers for good luck.

One second.

IN ANOTHER LIFE

He wasn't sure what his *actual* name was, or if he had ever even had one. Nor was he sure if his existence had ever been more than what it was now. He had lived too many lives, and he had died too many deaths, to be sure of anything, past that today his name was Steve, and that tomorrow it wouldn't be.

"Steve. Steven? You have to get up."

She sounded pretty. *Well, that's a bonus.*

'Steve' didn't want to get up. He rarely did want to. 'Steve' really didn't see the point. Despite this, he slowly and reluctantly opened his eyes to another day.

She *was* pretty and, not for the first time, 'Steve' found himself wishing that he had more time. Curly brunette hair, freckles—hers was a face far more pleasant than the fat, greasy jailor's he had awoken to yesterday.

"You really slept in!" she laughed. "You must have had quite the night!"

She didn't seem to be judging. Theirs must be a young relationship, not yet embittered by each other's every vice. And, it seemed to him, that he definitely had at least some of those. Suffering from what felt like a kick in the head, 'Steve' (realising that what he was experiencing must be the mother of all hangovers) slapped his hand to his forehead in quiet agony.

"Sleep well?" she asked with a knowing smile while tracing a finger across his chest.

"Oh, I completely died," 'Steve' said grimly.

He had.

Over breakfast 'Steve' slowly began to remember—or *learn*—his life. He had work today. Some kind of technical job at "the plant". He had no actual idea what "the plant" was, or what his job there was, or what it would involve— but it would come to him.

His head was still throbbing, and neither Panadol nor coffee did anything to dull the pounding veins that throbbed, physically visible, on his forehead. He *must* have had a night, and though he was annoyed by the evening prior that was clearly responsible for his morning's suffering, he was far less annoyed by it, than by the string of rapes and murders that had ruined his yesterday.

It was time for work, he knew, and the cute girl, Mary, moved to kiss him goodbye. She pulled him in closer—there was tongue—then, playfully pushing him away, she delivered a pat on the butt that directed him towards the door. 'Steve' could now vividly remember her, and found himself wishing again that there was more time. *There was never enough time.*

'Steve' got into his car and began his long drive to work. He could recall having driven it countless times, but this was his first time *actually* doing it himself. A left turn, a right turn, left onto the highway, an intersection, a green light (his right of way), a blur from the corner of his vision. A collision.

At eighty kilometres per hour another car's inattentive or careless driver had run a red, and slammed directly into the back right-hand side of 'Steve's' car. His vehicle rolled multiple times, smashing in the doors and making them unopenable. 'Steve' found himself hanging upside down, his car on its roof on an embankment. There was a spark—there must have been leaking fuel. The vehicle caught alight, and 'Steve' burned to death.

There was never enough time.

"Honey? Honey! Roger?!"

He sat up and blinked. She was very skinny, and he was very fat. The room smelt of dust and sweat.

"What's wrong, Roger? You were burning up! Was it a nightmare?"

He often wondered.

'Roger' grunted his way out of bed. Bad knees, laboured breath—he sweated from just partaking in the short walk from the bed to the bathroom. His life started to come back to him, fuzzy and uncertain.

He was 'Roger': fifty-five years old, worked at a used-car lot, eight kids, countless health issues.

Really lucked out with this one, 'Roger'.

'Roger' stepped into the bathroom and found that his socks were wet. He flicked on the light switch and felt his hair stand on end.

Loose wire? Flooded floor? Cooking flesh.

'Roger' was dead. It had only been about forty-five seconds since he had woken up.

He had died in under a minute. *That must be some kind of record.*

The next day his name was Kevin. 'Kevin' was trying to get fit. He had been eating healthy—or at the very least he had been eating *healthier*. He had even been going out on daily walks.

He was, however, not ready for the city-to-bay marathon. 'Kevin' had fallen over, grasping at his chest, and was dead before the paramedics had even heard the call.

Didn't even make it halfway.

He awoke again. He was lying in a double bed and could feel a warm body beside him. He couldn't yet remember his name, but it was slowly coming to him like objects in the mist. Justin? James? Joseph?—*it didn't matter.*

For as long as he could remember it had always been like this. Every morning he would awake into a new body. Not *new* new but new to him. He would slowly remember—or acquire—the memories of the body in which he now resided, until it felt *almost* as if it were his own. And then, sometime before midnight, he would be killed (or die in some fashion), only to awaken again the next morning in a new body, and the process goes on—

and on, and on, and on, and on.

He could not count how many times it had happened, nor could he recall a life before *this*. So far as he knew, this had *always* been his existence. He knew not what, nor why, it was—though he often wondered. *Was he cursed? Damned?* If he was cursed or damned he could no longer recall for what he was being punished. Nor could he ever spend much time dwelling on it. While the memories of his new body settled as each morning unfolded, the existential questions of his existence were quickly eclipsed by the daily life of the person he had become.

He had no chance to reflect on his own reality, nor did he have much chance to enjoy the short-lived normality of those lives that he encroached upon, before death so quickly caught him.

There was never enough time.

"Hey, you awake?" She sounded young and sad.

He flexed his muscles and curled his toes—he was young and fit again, probably in his mid-twenties.

"Yeah," he slowly responded. "I'm awake."

She was thin and pale like a porcelain doll, and looked maybe just as fragile. They both made their way to the kitchen, not bothering to get dressed further than the undergarments that they had evidently slept in. They sat at the small round table across from each other, neither taking the initiative to brew coffee or make breakfast.

His identity was slowly coming back to him; he was a student, studying... *something*. His university was someplace nearby.

"What's your name?" she asked, sounding vaguely disinterested.

The question threw him for a loop. He didn't yet know his name. Usually when he woke up alone it didn't matter how quickly he remembered the details of his life, and when he woke up with another person he would "fake it until he made it", taking cues from the partner. Never before had he been asked his name before he knew it.

Why wouldn't she know my name?

"Hello?" She was eyeing him strangely.

"Y-you don't know?" he sputtered.

"I really don't." She yawned.

He blushed with remembrance. This had been a one-night stand. Fortunately, with that recollection, so too came his name.

"Jarred." He jokingly extended a hand in introduction, wishing that it were not really the first time he had met her, and somewhat jealous of the unexperienced memories he was now recollecting from the night prior. She shook it, but did not laugh.

'Jarred' still could not recall her name but, as it was a one-night stand, he figured that it may be something his memory would not reveal to him anyway.

"Sorry, what was your name?" he asked.

"Umm..." She blinked.

She didn't know.

She began to rant:

"I haven't remembered yet."

"You see, I don't always wake up in the same place."

"Or body."

"I'm not sure who I—"

"What I—am."

"It sounds crazy."

"I sound crazy."

She fell silent.

'Jarred' smiled.

They were one and the same. He didn't know or even think that there was anyone else like him. He felt a strange mixture of both relief for himself, but also pity for her. He knew her suffering, as her suffering was his own. He hadn't yet said anything when she interrupted his thoughts as she began again:

"You think I'm mad, don't you? Fine. Forget it. I remember now. I'm 'Mandy', and I have to go meet with my mother."

'Mandy' got up to leave, and 'Jarred' grabbed her arm.

"Yesterday I died of a heart attack while jogging," he said.

She blinked again. "And before that?"

"I was electrocuted as a fat man named 'Roger'."

"And—"

"Car crash. Before that, lethal injection."

'Mandy' sat back down.

"You're serious, aren't you?"

"Yes."

"You die each day, and wake as someone else?" 'Mandy' asked, her eyes narrowed and serious.

"I—Yes, I do. I—" 'Jarred' began to trail off, distracted from the conversation. He looked at the wall clock, suddenly realising the time. He would soon be late for class. He had finals coming—something that suddenly felt extremely important to him. As it always did, the compulsion to follow the life in which he had been inserted was growing over- whelming. Never before had he felt a desire to fight it as he did now. He struggled to his feet, legs shaking, "I'll have to go now. I'll be late for class."

She softly took his hand and, in a gentle but firm tone, told him "no".

'Jarred' sat back down. He concentrated on trying to remember what they had been talking of before, and trying to force his concerns about finals out of his mind.

"Yes," he began again. "Each day I die and awake as another," he finally answered her question from minutes prior.

"Are we the only ones?"

"I thought I was the only one."

"We really should go," she said, looking at the time. 'Mandy' stood and walked into the bedroom. Slowly she picked up her scattered clothing and began to dress.

'Jarred' did the same. He pulled his shirt over his head, and then turned back to 'Mandy'. "Have you ever not... followed?"

He wasn't sure how to word it, but she seemed to know exactly what he meant. She sat on the bed.

"No. It calls—I can't... and I hate it. But maybe together...?"

'Jarred' could see the bedside clock behind her. Class would start in five minutes: he would be marked as absent, and his grade would be affected. He forced a laugh that came out more manic than he had intended.

"It is so stupid: their lives—*our lives*—seem so important to us. We're only them for a day!" he sat beside her.

"You know, I haven't—*Mandy* hasn't paid her taxes? It's a little worry that's eating at the back of her—*my*—mind. Why should I care? Mandy will be dead by the end of the day, and *I'll* be someone else!"

'Jarred' nodded furiously. "I'm worried about being unprepared for exams. Exams are a week away, and I'm dead tonight!"

"*Jarred* is dead tonight," she corrected.

"So, who—*what*—are we, if I'm not Jarred?"

"All of them; none of them. Something else?" she paused. "I don't know," she admitted.

She stood and walked out of the bedroom, and down the hallway. 'Jarred' followed. As they reached the kitchen 'Jarred' caught her hand. 'Mandy' stopped, checked herself, and then laughed awkwardly, sitting back down at the table.

"I didn't mean to—It's just that I'm supposed to meet with my—*her*—mother."

'Jarred' nodded sympathetically. "What if we try to focus on something else, other than what we're supposed to be doing?"

"What else is there?" she said, sounding defeated.

"How much memory do you retain of the previous day—life?"

"Fragments. Death, mainly. Their memories always fade fast, replaced by the new ones. If whatever is left is me... then I'm not much." She sounded depressed, and then absent-mindedly added, "I really *should* call my mother."

A smile crossed over 'Jarred's' mouth. "I got eaten by a lion once," he said.

She laughed, "No way!"

"Yup. I was supposed to be feeding it—I guess I did!"

She laughed again. "I drowned in a capsizing boat—get this—while we were watching *The Poseidon Adventure* in the cruise ship's onboard movie theatre!"

"Oh, how very simpatico! I was a stuntman at one point, you know?"

"Were you any good?"

"Not good enough to hit my mark, apparently!"

"Oh no!" she smiled.

They talked for hours, exchanging tales of the most bizarre lives and deaths that they could remember. This was the kind of morbid conversation only those who had died 365 times a year could share. 'Jarred' enjoyed it, in a strange way. It was nice to be able to share a moment he thought no-one could ever understand with someone. But it was getting late; the sun had gone down, and class was well and truly over.

'Mandy' scribbled something onto a piece of paper and slid it to him. "I'm sorry. There's never enough time... I really do have to go; I have work. But I don't want this to be a one-night stand. Contact me."

'Jarred' took the piece of paper and read it carefully. It was an email address. He wrote his own email down in response, and handed it over. He noticed the time on the microwave's clock with a start, and realised that he too would be late for work soon. Walking her to the door, he kissed her cheek, and she left.

It wasn't until she was three steps down the path that 'Jarred' realised what was happening and snapped out of it. "Fight it, 'Mandy'! Come back!" he shouted.

She paused. Her shoulders slumped. And then she turned and walked back into the house looking stricken.

"I hate it. I really hate it. I didn't even know I had succumbed—it just felt so *natural*... What if I am nothing else, but what I become each day?" She sounded exhausted.

'Jarred' kissed her again and, for the first time, it was because he wanted to, not because who he was today wanted to.

"I didn't think I was anything else but the longer I fight it, the more I feel like *me*, rather than *them*," 'Jarred' responded.

"But what about tomorrow? We'll just be someone else again. You may wake up in Paris; I might wake up in New Zealand! And before long, Jarred's and Mandy's memories will fade and be replaced!"

A glimmer of hope washed over 'Jarred' as something suddenly occurred to him: "Or... maybe you will wake up as 'Mandy', and I'll wake up as 'Jarred'... For all we know we might have already supposed to have died. I've never gone against their lives before. We may have missed their deaths in doing so... and if we don't die, do we still wake up as someone else?"

She pressed herself against him. "I hope that's the case. I don't want to wake up without you."

He squeezed her. He didn't want that either, and so together they went to bed.

'Twenty-eight year old Mandy Anders and twenty-two year old Jarred Austin were found dead this morning in Jarred's home. Police searched the premises after Mandy's mother reported her missing. There were no obvious indications of the cause of death, but police are treating the situation as suspicious.'

He groaned loudly and slapped the radio-alarm clock off the bedside table. He knew exactly what the cause of death was. *A cruel curse*—some form of hateful fate that chose to show him the prospect of true happiness only so that it could have something more to take from him.

"Mornin', birthday boy; excited for skydiving?!"

He laughed hysterically at the question. *Plummeting to my death, that's a new one!* he thought darkly.

Quickly and reluctantly 'Ben' began to learn all that he needed to know of his new life, but for the first time ever he fought every piece of knowledge that came his way. He didn't want to know what Ben's favourite colour was. Or what Ben's girlfriend's name was. Or what position Ben played in gridiron. He wanted to remember the yesterday that he had spent with 'Mandy'—the only life he had lived thus far that had felt like he was truly living.

The previous day's memories quickly began to fade, and 'Ben' grasped at any detail he could retain. He and his new partner, whatever-her-name-was, were in a car now on the way to the airstrip. He answered her questions like a robot, not engaging with their dialogue on any intellectual level, instead focusing on any memory he could conjure with 'Mandy'. It was like trying to catch smoke in his hand. Puff by puff it escaped.

'Mandy's' face?

Gone.

Her laugh?

Fading.

There was never enough time.

Her touch?

Forgotten.

Her email? Nothing but a blur.

His email... his... email.

They had stepped onto the plane now, and all of 'Ben's' focus concentrated on one last piece of information that was attempting to evade him.

What *had* Jarred's email been?

He could distinctly remember having written it down. 'Ben' closed his eyes and envisioned himself having done so. It clicked.

Quickly he got out his—*Ben's*—phone. There was still service. He logged out of Ben's email, and logged into Jarred's. The password was tricky. He hadn't written *that* down, but there was a kind of residual muscle memory, and after four desperate attempts he entered it correctly.

There was one new email. Received from a 'Mandy Anders' at 7 am that morning. *Several hours after they had both died.* It read:

> *Today I am a young librarian in London. How, I wonder, does a young librarian find themselves dead? Guess I'll find out before long! Are you nearby? I hope we can meet—if not today, then soon.*

Hands shaking, 'Ben' hit *reply.*

> *My dear Mandy. It is my birthday today, and I am about to go skydiving in Austin, Texas. (Three guesses how this will end.) I'll message you from the ground (if I don't arrive there too fast). I don't see myself getting to London, but maybe we'll be closer tomorrow.*
>
> *I will see you again—if not in this life, then the next, or the many more that follow. We will meet again.*
>
> *We have all the time in the world.*

'Ben' hit *send.* The door to the plane had been opened. With a smile, he pocketed the phone, and jumped.

CONTACT THE AUTHOR

Email:

darkwellbled@outlook.com

Twitter:

@DarkwellBled